JANET RENO
United States
Attorney General

—PEOPLE TO KNOW—

JANET RENO
United States Attorney General

Virginia Meachum

ENSLOW PUBLISHERS, INC.
44 Fadem Rd.   P.O. Box 38
Box 699   Aldershot
Springfield, N.J. 07081   Hants GU12 6BP
U.S.A.   U.K.

Copyright ©1995 by Virginia Meachum

All rights reserved.

No part of this book may be reproduced by any means without the written permission of the publisher.

Library of Congress Cataloging-in-Publication Data

Meachum, Virginia.
 Janet Reno: United States Attorney General / Virginia Meachum.
    p. cm. — (People to know)
  Includes bibliographical references and index.
  ISBN 0-89490-549-X
  1. Reno, Janet, 1938—Juvenile literature. 2. Attorneys general—United States—Biography—Juvenile literature. [1. Reno, Janet, 1938-   . 2. Attorneys general. 3. Women—Biography.] I. Title. II. Series.
KF373.R45M43 1994
353.5'092—dc20   94-27995
[B]   CIP
                                                              AC

Printed in the United States of America

10 9 8 7 6 5 4 3 2 1

Illustration Credits:
Clyde Butcher, p. 15; Coral Gables High School, p. 22; Courtesy of the Reno Family, pp. 17, 32; Florida State Archives, pp. 44, 50, 106; Harvard Law School, p. 34; *The Miami Herald,* pp. 21, 39, 54; Reuters/Bettmann, p. 70; United States Department of Justice, pp. 6, 80, 83, 86, 98, 103, 109; Washington, D.C., Convention and Visitors Association, pp. 62, 66, 88.

Cover Illustration:
United States Department of Justice

Contents

1 The President's Choice 7
2 Everglades Childhood 11
3 Career Decision 25
4 Finding a Place in Law 37
5 Making a Difference 49
6 Answering the Call 59
7 A Full Agenda 73
8 Curbing Violence 91
9 Her Two Worlds 101
   A Message From Janet Reno
      to America's Young People 115
   Chronology 116
   Chapter Notes 118
   Further Reading 126
   Index 127

Janet Reno

1

The President's Choice

On a Friday morning in early March 1993, a tall, stately woman waited inside the Roosevelt Room of the White House, near the President's Oval Office. An air of anticipation and excitement surrounded her. Janet Reno was soon to be sworn in as United States attorney general. She would be the first woman in the nation's history to hold this responsible position.

The attorney general is head of the Department of Justice, and is the chief law enforcement officer of the United States. Appointed by the President, he or she is a member of the President's Cabinet, and provides legal advice to the President. The attorney general is responsible for the internal security of the nation, and that includes guarding the safety of national secrets.

What kind of person would be qualified to take on

this monumental task? Who would be that knowledgeable, that strong in character, fair in judgment, and that dedicated to providing justice for all of the United States citizens?

President Bill Clinton chose Janet Reno. At a news conference in the White House Rose Garden on February 11, 1993, the President named the fifty-four-year-old Miami prosecutor as his nominee for attorney general.

Why did the President choose Janet Reno? At this time, crime and violence had become a major problem in the United States. The President needed an attorney general who could speak and act authoritatively on crime. He needed someone with an extensive background in the criminal justice system.

Janet Reno filled that need. For the past fifteen years, she had been the state attorney for Dade County, Florida. This area, which includes Miami, was known for violent crime, drug activity, and racial conflict. As chief prosecutor, she handled thousands of criminal cases.[1] She was recognized not only for toughness in providing justice for crime victims, but for her compassionate judgment. Her reputation for integrity and hard work, as well as her record for success, made her a highly favorable nominee. In addition, his choice of Janet Reno enabled President Clinton to honor his goal of nominating the first woman attorney general.

After that press conference in February at the White

House, the next step on the road to confirmation was the Senate Judiciary Committee hearings. On March 9, Reno appeared before the committee to be questioned about her past performance and personal philosophy. On that first day of the hearings, Reno's opening statement reflected her strength of character.

Speaking of her simple upbringing in Florida, she told of the log-and-stone house her parents had laboriously built by themselves. "That house is a symbol to me that you can do anything you really want to, if it is the right thing to do, and you put your mind to it."[2]

During long hours of questioning by committee members, many issues on crime were presented for her opinion. In her replies, Janet Reno expressed support for strong gun control laws and for social programs to keep children from turning to crime; she also emphasized the need for tough, certain punishment of hardened criminals.

After only two days of hearings, the committee unanimously favorable recommendation to the Senate. On the following day, with many glowing tributes, the full Senate confirmed her nomination in a 98 to 0 vote.[3]

And now, on this Friday morning of March 12, 1993, relatives, friends, and members of Congress joined tall, stately Janet Reno to witness her official swearing-in ceremony.

President Clinton stood with her. A young niece, whose name also is Janet Reno, held the Bible. With her right hand raised, and her left on the Bible, Reno clearly and firmly repeated the words of Supreme Court Justice Byron R. White, as he administered the oath of office:[4]

> I, Janet Reno, do solemnly swear that I will faithfully execute the Office of Attorney General of the United States, and will to the best of my ability preserve, protect, and defend the Constitution of the United States.[5]

Amid the applause which followed, Reno's generous smile expressed her great joy and pride.

The United States had acquired its first woman attorney general. Her judgment would be tested many times. Her decisions would be of vital and far-reaching importance. But she appeared eager to meet the challenge.

"It's an extraordinary experience," she said. "I hope I do the women of America proud."[6]

Everglades Childhood

In Miami, Florida, on July 21, 1938, Jane and Henry Reno became the parents of a baby girl. They named her Janet. Her mother chose the name Janet because it meant "Little Jane."[1] How could they know then how tall "Little Jane" would grow, and in how many ways?

Janet's parents were both journalists. Henry Reno, a gentle, Danish immigrant, worked as a police reporter for the *Miami Herald*. Jane Wood Reno, energetic and outspoken, was an investigative reporter for the *Miami News*. Earlier, her first full-time job had been writing obituaries for the same newspaper as Henry. Their fondness for nature and outdoor adventure brought them together on a "first date"—crawfishing in the Florida Keys from Henry's small boat. Before long, they married and moved into a small house in the Coconut Grove area of Miami.

This was to become young Janet's first home. Here each year, another child was born to the Renos until there was Robert, Maggy, and Mark, as well as Janet. Needing more space, the family moved to a larger house in South Miami, with a generous yard. Within a short time, they planted a garden and acquired a goat, chickens, a cow, and assorted pets.

When the four children reached school age, their father bought twenty-one acres of undeveloped land in South Dade County, near the Everglades. He wanted his family to enjoy the freedom of country living.

But first they needed a house. Since their funds were invested in the land, there was no money left to hire a builder. Reno's mother—strong and loving a challenge—solved the problem. With Henry Reno at work all day and the children in school, *she* would build the house.

And so, in a clearing on this vast acreage of heavy tropical growth, she set about digging a trench for the foundation to be poured. Then, by watching experts and by reading how-to books, she learned to lay concrete blocks, hoist timber into place, lay bricks, and install wiring and plumbing. In two years, with occasional help from her husband and the children, Jane Reno finished their house. It was a sturdy house with a cedar-beamed ceiling, brick floor, spacious rooms, and a long screened porch. This is where Janet and her sister and brothers would spend their childhood. Except for her years away at college, this is where Janet Reno would continue to live until her appointment as attorney general.

The family now lived so far out from the city that they had few neighbors, few conveniences, and no telephone. To keep in touch with its police reporter, the *Miami Herald* had to persuade Southern Bell to string a telephone line beyond the city limits to this remote house.

The Renos were excited about the natural environment around them. Now they had ample space for all the animals they enjoyed. Another cow was added, then goats, pigs, ponies, and a basset hound who kept them well supplied with pups. Reno's mother once brought home two peacock eggs to be hatched, and named them both Horace. As time went on, a colorful array of peacocks and peahens strutted about the lawn—all named Horace. Various wildlife was apt to show up anytime—raccoons, pelicans, macaws, snakes—which, if not too offensive, were welcome to stay.

Of course, there were chores to be done. When home from school, the children all pitched in—caring for the animals, clearing the fast-growing holly, mowing grass, sawing wood for the fireplace. But on weekends and school vacations, the Renos spent many hours exploring the nearby Everglades.

The Everglades area of southern Florida is one of the

largest swamplands in the world. It covers 5,000 square miles from Lake Okeechobee in the north to almost the tip of the Florida peninsula.[2] Much of the Everglades looks like a vast field of grain waving in the breeze. Actually, it is a vast expanse of fresh water, about six inches deep, flowing slowly through tall saw grass on its way to the sea. Now and then an island of trees, ferns, and flowers can be seen, and thickets of mangroves abound near the coast. Cypress trees, Southern pine, and palms are native to this area, and it is home to bobcats, otters, exotic birds, reptiles, and other marshland creatures.

Janet, Maggy, Robert, and Mark hiked through dense saw grass, climbed over tangled undergrowth, and paddled their canoes through uncharted streams—ideal nesting places for alligators. Led by their fearless mother, they fished, swam with turtles, and camped under the stars.

Once while exploring the Tamiami Trail, they came upon a camp of Native Americans—the Miccosukee, a tribe of the Seminoles. Miccosukees live in chickee huts—open-sided homes on wooden platforms, raised above the swampland, and roofed with palm thatch. In the marsh clearings, they grow vegetables and keep chickens, pigs, and cows. Many of the men hunt and fish. A camp or village draws together the members of one family, and its married daughters, their husbands and children.[3]

A cypress tree in Gaskin Bay of the Everglades. Janet's mother used cypress wood to build their house.

The Renos quickly formed a friendship with this family, the Osceolas, that was to last through the years. They taught Janet's mother how to wrestle an alligator, and stew turtles over a fire pit. They shared much of their unique culture with Janet and her sister and brothers. Later, when Jane Wood Reno returned to work for the *Miami News*, she wrote a story about the Miccosukees, which helped them to acquire a school for their children. In grateful triumph, they celebrated with a special ceremony, and awarded Jane Wood Reno the honorary title of "Miccosukee Princess."[4]

Daily life in the Reno home was carried on with few conveniences. There was no hot water heater, no washer, dryer, or air conditioner. But here in the early 1950s, the family accepted this lack of household aids as a natural part of a rural setting. They lived simply, but fully. Janet's mother taught her to milk a cow, churn butter, bake a cake. She taught her to recite the poetry of Coleridge, to appreciate the works of Shakespeare, to enjoy a Beethoven symphony.

When television became an addition in most homes, the Renos had none. Janet's mother said it led to "mind rot." But the family did not lack for worldly information. A steady diet of news came from radio, newspapers, and on-the-spot tales brought home by Henry Reno from his daily round of crime reporting. With floor-to-ceiling shelves of books in the study, reading was a frequent pastime. And, although the

Janet enjoyed outdoor sports. Living far from others, the Reno children played most games together.

family followed no formal religion, they all studied the Bible.

Another pastime was debate. They all had strong opinions, and none were shy about expressing them. A friend once said that, in the Reno household, debate was a varsity sport. Perhaps these early years of matching wits with her sister, brothers, and quick-thinking parents, developed Janet's ability to form and express her own opinions fearlessly.

Or did she already have that ability? As a child, one of her greatest dislikes was having to wear shoes. Once in a burst of defiance, she declared that she was going to be a lawyer because she did not want anybody telling her what to do.[5]

Little was forbidden by Janet's parents, but the line between right and wrong was well-defined. Maggy recalls, "We couldn't lie, cheat, steal, or hurt people littler than us."[6] And Janet agrees, referring to her mother, "She spanked us hard, and she loved us with all her heart."[7]

Janet's home life, immersed in the outdoors and wildlife, was a sharp contrast to the bustling city where her father went to work each day, and where she went to school. The children were driven the long distance to school by their father—in a red Jeep—on his way to work. After school, they were picked up by their mother in her yellow Jeep. "But the yellow Jeep had no top," says Maggy. "On rainy days, we arrived home thoroughly soaked!"[8]

As the oldest of four children, Janet had always been the leader of any activity. In school, she fell easily into the role of organizing and leading in both classroom and playground activity. In fact, her take-charge manner became so evident that her fifth-grade teacher called her "bossy."[9] But she was well-liked by her classmates. One of her teachers remembers that Janet would always be among the first chosen for a team. However, if someone was left out, she would quickly give up her place to that child.

By the time Janet reached junior high school, she was the tallest girl in class—five feet eleven inches—and still growing. Although conscious of her height, she did not let it discourage her from participating in the activities which drew her interest. One of these was a class in ballroom dancing and manners. It seemed to represent the polite world of her maternal grandmother, Daisy Sloan Hunter Wood.

Unlike Janet's mother, this sedate Southern lady dressed impeccably, never raised her voice, and lived in quiet elegance among family treasures. It was a world far different from her own. Sometime later, sensitive to her granddaughter's feelings, Grandmother Wood passed along to Janet an heirloom four-poster bed and a large oriental rug. Janet's room was now a striking contrast to the bare floors and rustic decor she had always known, and it pleased her. Other than her parents, it was this gracious lady who impressed Janet Reno the most during her growing-up years. "My grandmother had a great capacity for making those around her feel like they were important, special, and beloved."[10]

When Janet was about thirteen, her mother arranged for her to spend a year in Germany. She was to live with a great-aunt and uncle—the latter being a military judge with the Allied High Commission. If this year abroad was meant to be a learning experience for Janet, it truly was. She learned the meaning of homesickness. "This was her first time to live away from home," says Maggy. "She really missed her family—and we missed her, too."[11]

Two aunts, both sisters of Janet's mother, also served with the military. Aunt Daisy Wood was a nurse and, during World War II, she accompanied General Patton's army in North Africa and its march on Italy. Aunt Winnie joined the Women's Air Force Service Pilots. Popularly known as WASPS, this corps of civilian flyers tested combat aircraft and trained men pilots. Toward the end of the war, Winnie came back to Miami and, with some fellow pilots, gave flying lessons. Young Janet was impressed. "I can do that," she told herself. "I can do anything I put my mind to."[12]

At Coral Gables Senior High School, Janet put her mind to many things. An excellent student, she was also active in numerous extracurricular activities. Besides

Janet Reno's mother and father welcome her back home from a year in Germany.

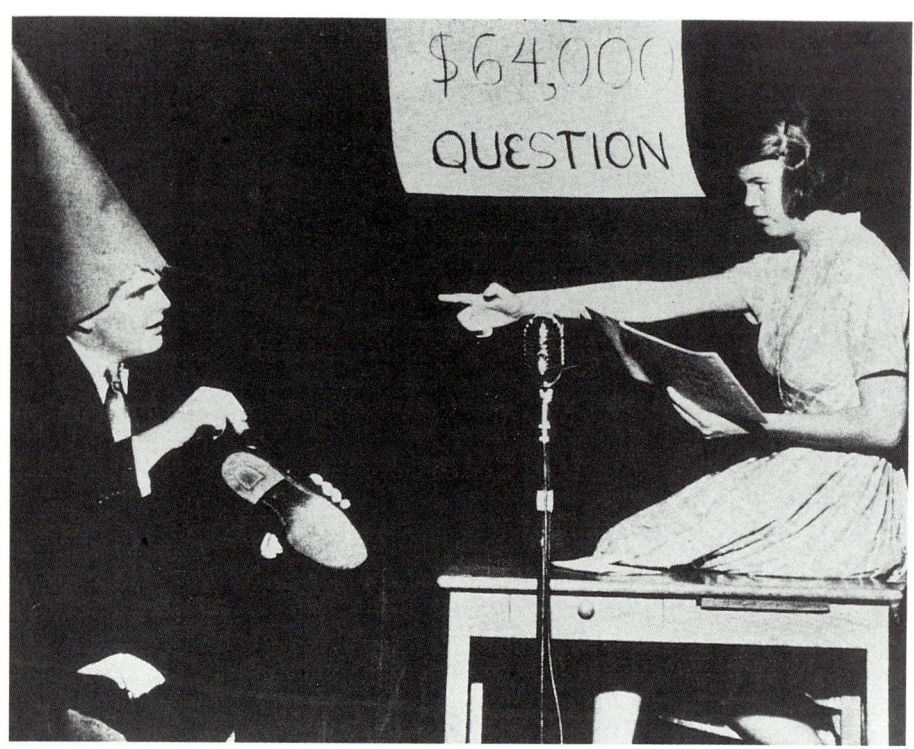

Janet performing a skit at Coral Gables High School. She was active in many extracurricular activities.

French Club and Varsity Debate, she was elected to the Student Council, and frequently represented her school at leadership conferences.

Janet was now over six feet tall and had become acutely self-conscious about her appearance. She tried not to stand up straight—always slumping forward. To find clothes that fit was an endless problem—especially when she preferred "dungarees" to dresses anyway. Although both parents were of average height, each of the Reno children grew to be more than six feet tall. According to Maggy, neither she nor Janet attended her senior prom because they were so much taller than all the boys.

Despite her self-consciousness, Janet continued gamely to pursue her interests. When Coral Gables Senior High began grooming students for the state Extemporaneous Speaking Contest, Janet became a participant. Her topic was "free trade," and she worked long hours doing research and preparing for the competition. Her effort was well rewarded. It was a moment of particular pride when she was declared the state high school winner. Perhaps she *could* do anything she put her mind to.

But soon Janet would be graduating. The time had come to think seriously about her plans for the future.

3

Career Decision

Janet Reno graduated, valedictorian, from Coral Gables Senior High School in June 1956. At various stages during childhood, she had dreamed of becoming a major-league baseball pitcher, a doctor, a rancher, a marine biologist, or a lawyer. Now it was time to make the big decision. Which path would she follow?

While in high school, a favorite subject of hers had been chemistry. This interest, along with a natural compassion for people, led her to decide on a career in medicine. In the fall, she would enter Cornell University in Ithaca, New York, as a premedical student. Why Cornell? Although Reno was aware of this university through an uncle who had attended, the choice was made after some serious thought. As she explains, "I wanted to go to a diverse school with an excellent academic standing, that was not in a big city."[1]

Meanwhile, she found a summer job in the Dade County Sheriff's Office. Her parents had sold off some of their land to pay for her tuition, but she needed to help with other college expenses. With four children in succession to send through college, the Renos would be under a financial strain for the next eight years.

In the fall, Reno arrived at Cornell University. Located high on a hill, the campus overlooks the city of Ithaca below as well as Lake Cayuga, one of the eleven Finger Lakes. These lakes were so named because they stretch out like the fingers of a hand.

As one of about 10,000 students at the university that year, Reno moved into Clara Dickson Hall, one of several residence halls for women. She was now 1,500 miles from home, and among strangers. Like that year spent in Germany, she would miss the daily camaraderie and support of her boisterous family. But once classes began, she would be swept up into this new world. Needing to find part-time work, she immediately signed on as a waitress in the residence dining hall. In this way, she soon became acquainted with many other students.

Reno was serious and hardworking. As the oldest child in her family, and the first to attend college, she wanted to do her best. Jane Wood Reno has been quoted as saying, "Good, better, best. Don't ever rest, until good is better and better is best."² But the Reno children knew that both of their parents expected them to do their best.

Taking a full load of classes, which required hours of study, and working part-time, did not allow for much social life. Also, Reno served as president of her dormitory, which brought problems to solve and group activities to plan.

With her natural interest in issues and doing something about them, she soon became involved in women's government. As in high school, she was not afraid to express her opinion and take a stand for what she believed in—traits which apparently won the admiration of her fellow students. During her junior year, Reno was elected president of the Women's Student Government Association. This group gave Cornell women control over certain policies concerning residence halls and sorority houses.

Despite this full schedule, Reno's classwork was not neglected. On two occasions, she received scholarship awards: the Ida H. Hyde Scholarship, and the Laura Osborne Memorial Scholarship. These awards were a welcome addition to her college fund. They also added to her self-esteem. Although she was never lacking in confidence, it was reassuring to be considered deserving of this recognition. In looking back, she has said, "This was a period when I began to think, 'You know—you really *can* do things.'"³

Life at Cornell broadened her experience and also

brought new perceptions. Although an honor student and well-liked, Reno was never taken into a sorority. This is not unusual on a college campus, but for an achiever who was generous in the acceptance of others, this could have been a disappointment. However, as Reno recalls, "It hurts . . . when you're rejected. It hurts a little." Then she adds, "But obviously, it didn't bother me too much. Some of the best friends I ever had were in sororities."[4]

Reno's qualities of leadership and fair-mindedness had become increasingly evident among those who knew her. A former classmate, Dale Rogers Marshall, who is now president of Wheaton College in Norton, Massachusetts, recently said, "Reno is a leader. . . . She stood out back then as very straightforward, someone with very clear opinions and very independent. She did not try to just go along with the group. Whatever the issue, she thought things out for herself."[5]

Each summer Reno returned home to catch up with her family, and to replenish her college fund by finding another job. Unknowingly, these summer jobs were helping to shape her future.

Working in the Public Safety Department at the Dade County Courthouse gave her a firsthand look at the judicial process. Working in the County Welfare's Psychiatric Placement Division convinced her that "you could be in government and not be bound by bureaucracy."[6] And while working in the lab at the Dade

Medical Institute, she became keenly aware of her ineptness with test tubes and lab technology. "I was a klutz in the laboratory," she said. "Worse than that, I was the sort of klutz who dropped things."[7] It was then she began to think about a change in her career.

Reno's satisfaction in helping others, along with her interest in chemistry had originally led her to major in premedicine. But now, she began to rethink her choice. Those summer jobs in Miami had exposed her to the real world—allowed her to actually witness what could be done to improve conditions for the less fortunate. Then, too, her campus experience as a leader in student government—reaching workable solutions through study and discussion—had appealed to her. Perhaps she ought to study law.

The subject was presented to her family. At first, Reno's mother was skeptical. In the early 1960s, it was rare for a woman to choose a career in law. If she chose it, the opportunity to be accepted as a practicing attorney was limited. Traditionally, law was a man's profession.

On thinking it over, however, Jane Wood Reno's fiercely independent nature won out. "You can do anything, be anything you really want to be, regardless of whether you're a woman," she told her daughter. "You want to be a lawyer? You can be a lawyer."[8]

Reno's father, in his crime-reporting work, had developed a respect for and friendship with many lawyers, who were often invited to visit at the Reno ranch. His response was to take his daughter to meet with a well-known Dade County judge. "Henry, this town has too many lawyers," said the judge. "But what it desperately needs is *good* lawyers. Go ahead, send her to law school."[9]

And then, there was her grandfather, George Washington Wood, Jr., who was himself a successful attorney. He, too, encouraged his granddaughter to pursue a career in law.

Reno listened to the input of others, and she listened to her own thoughts. Law had the power to solve problems. It had the power to correct injustice. She admired that.

And so, Janet Reno did what seemed right for her. She applied for admission to Harvard Law School. She had heard it was the best.

Admission to law school is competitive, and the application process is time-consuming and expensive. Any person interested in entering law school must take the Law School Admissions Test (LSAT). This is a four-hour exam, nationally administered at certain locations. It is designed to measure some of the mental qualities needed to be successful in studying law. The score made on this test is one of the factors in considering an applicant for law school admission.[10]

Other steps in applying for admission include filling out an application form, a personal statement form, a college certification form, and acquiring letters of recommendation.[11]

After Reno completed all of the requirements, her request then merged with several hundred others to be carefully studied by the admissions committee. What are the qualities Harvard Law School looks for in deciding on an applicant? Most students who are admitted are in the top 10 percent of their college class, have high LSAT scores, and have had "substantial accomplishments" in work or outside activities. Personal qualities such as "energy, ambition, sound judgment, and high ideals" are also considered in a decision on an applicant.[12]

Typically, it takes four to eight weeks for the admissions committee to reach a decision. Those are anxious weeks of waiting—hoping for a favorable reply. When the reply finally arrived for Reno, it was favorable! Delighted, she announced the good news. Her once skeptical mother "whooped with joy." "I guess that's what I always wanted to do," she said. And Grandfather Wood drawled, "Aw, honey, I knew you could do that."[13]

In the spring of 1960, Janet Reno graduated from Cornell with a Bachelor of Arts degree in chemistry. That fall, she went on to law school in Cambridge, Massachusetts.

Harvard Law School is located on the main campus of Harvard University, across the Charles River from Boston. Founded in 1817, it is the oldest, largest, and

Janet Reno graduated from Cornell University in 1960, with a Bachelor of Arts degree in chemistry. In the fall, she entered Harvard Law School.

one of the most esteemed of America's law schools. Getting accepted here has always been an achievement. For women, getting accepted into this prestigious school was unheard of until 1949. The first women ever—twelve in number—graduated in 1953.

Seven years later, Janet Reno was one of only sixteen women enrolled in the class of five hundred and forty-four. In this select group of quality students, would she be able to survive the demanding work and classroom competition that lay ahead? "You can be anything you want to be," her mother had said. Surely, this would be the test.

First-year students at Harvard Law School learn to do legal research, write briefs, and deliver oral arguments. The five courses required of all freshmen are Torts, Contracts, Property, Criminal Law, and Civil Procedure.[14] Most of these subjects are taught using the case method. That is, an actual problem that a client might bring to a lawyer is presented, and the class must provide the legal advice to solve it. In general, a class consists of from forty-five to seventy students, each prepared to present his or her own solution to the problem.

For Reno, the days rushed by in a whirl of classes, hours of research in the immense law school library, and intense preparation for each day's legal problems and oral arguments. Here, as at Cornell, she worked part-time to help with expenses—doing a research

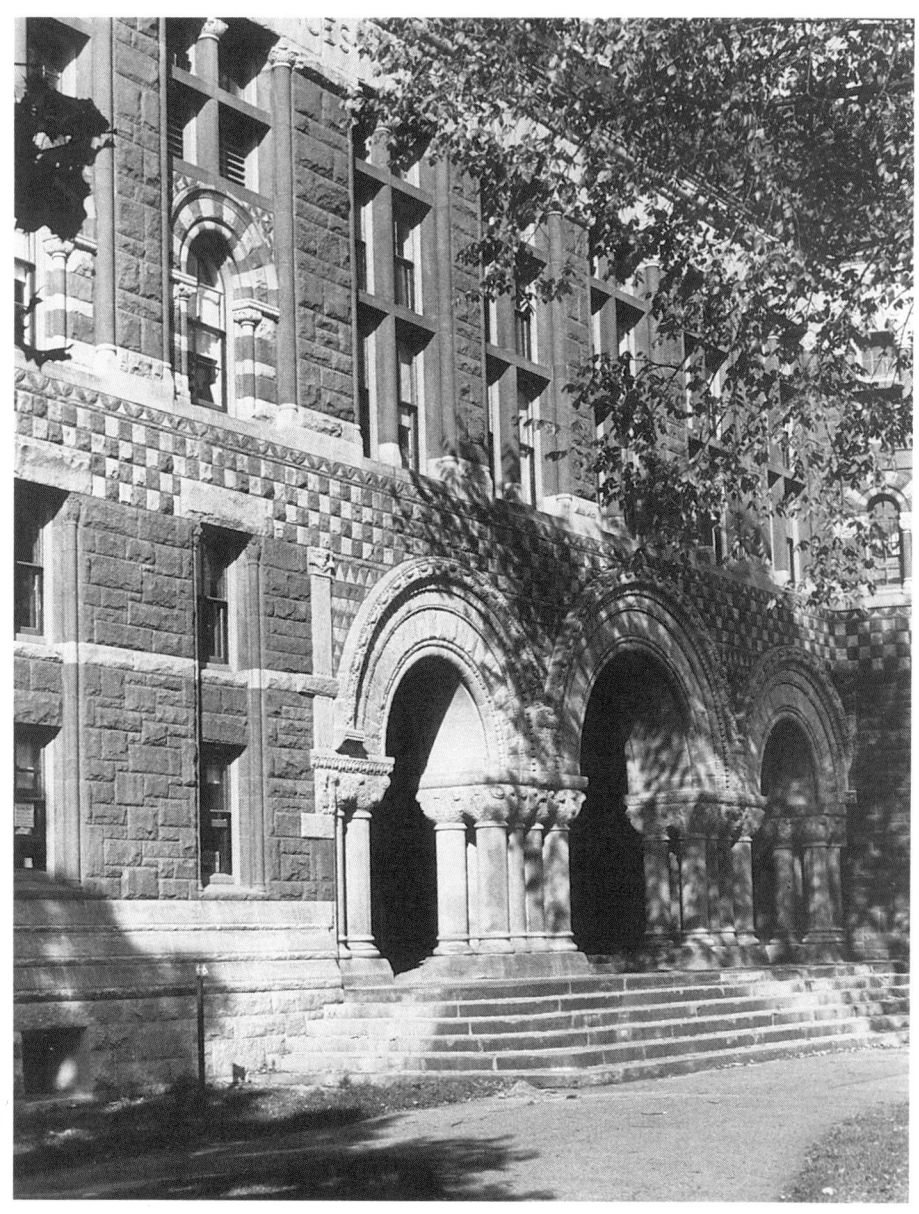

Austin Hall, a classroom building at Harvard Law School, from which Janet Reno graduated in 1963.

project for a law school professor. There was little time for other campus activities.

Social life for Reno was not a priority, but she did feel accepted by her classmates. On looking back, she said, "I was rarely invited to dinner or anything . . . but I didn't feel like an outcast. I don't think I'm a gregarious person, in the sense of having a lot of casual friends."[15] Clearly, she was there as a student—to learn to think, consider opposing views, and come up with answers.

Her goal was to prepare for a career in law. Reno's first brush with discrimination came the summer between her junior and senior years. Returning to Miami, she applied for work in a prominent Miami law firm and was turned down. When asked recently how she felt about this, Reno replied, "I felt mad." And what did she do next? "Went and got a job in another law firm. I never let it bother me after that."[16] It is interesting to note that, fourteen years later, the same firm that had rejected her made her a partner.

Reflecting on those three years in law school, Janet Reno said, "Harvard Law School was the best educational experience I ever had. . . . I believe that the way I approach problems—taking them apart and putting them back together again—is due to the training I got from some extraordinary professors."[17]

By the end of her third and final year, Reno had experience in the handling of cases in court, drafting lawsuits, and working with professionals on actual cases in family law, welfare, and mental health.

In June 1963, she, along with five hundred others, marched in procession to receive her well-earned degree in law, an LL.B.

True to her parents, Janet Reno had done her best. Now it was time to find her place in law.

4

Finding a Place in Law

Janet Reno returned to Miami where she planned to practice law. But even as a Harvard-trained lawyer, she had difficulty getting started. Not only was she a beginner in the profession, but most large law firms were apprehensive about accepting a woman associate. The appearance of a woman arguing a case in the courtroom was still somewhat of an oddity. With persistence, she was finally accepted in the smaller firm of Brigham and Brigham, where she began to gain some basic legal experience.

In 1967, Reno and her family suffered a deep personal loss in the sudden death of her father. Henry Reno had recently retired from forty-three years of reporting for the *Miami Herald*, when he had a fatal heart attack. Janet Reno had always been a strong admirer of her father. She often says it was from him that she acquired a compassion for people. "He always looked at people with respect and dignity. He tried to see the best in people."[1]

Reno continued in private practice, but was soon to become interested in politics. In 1967, the U.S. Supreme Court ordered Florida's state legislature to be reapportioned to reflect the growth in population. This increased the number of senators and representatives needed from Dade County to serve in the state capital.

Gerald Lewis, a friend of Reno's from Harvard Law School, decided to run for one of the new seats available in the state House of Representatives. Wanting to help, she became his campaign manager. She recruited a corps of energetic volunteers and led them in a vigorous campaign. By the time Lewis won as state representative, Reno had become well-known in the political community for her strength and reliability. She now became the junior partner in the firm of Lewis and Reno.

When another of Miami's new legislators, Representative Talbot "Sandy" D'Alemberte, became Chairman of the Judiciary Committee in 1971, he asked Reno to become his staff director. Numerous changes were needed to update the court system, and the job would be an enormous challenge. "I was looking for someone strong enough to take on the world," he said.[2]

This was Reno's first political appointment. "The

Janet Reno in the private practice of law, early in her career.

world" she took on was the task of modernizing the state of Florida's court system, and she plunged in with customary zeal. After months of in-depth study, she drafted a revision of the state constitution, which would make possible the reorganization of the former outdated system. Among the many changes, it provided for the elimination of justices of the peace, constables, and municipal courts—which were no longer an efficient way to serve the vastly increased population. Many people opposed these changes, but Reno was convincing. When voters finally approved the proposed revision, she gained many admirers among the legislators.

Reno now decided to run for election to a seat in the state House. By representing the public, she would be serving the public. That appealed to her. But several factors weakened her electability.

At this time, Janet Reno was not widely known by the general public of Dade County. Also, in addition to conducting her own campaign, much of her energy went into helping friends with their campaigns. And, she was backing Democratic presidential candidate George McGovern, a U.S. senator from South Dakota. McGovern was not completely trusted by the majority of voters. His proposals, including his opposition to the Vietnam War, were looked upon as too far left for most Americans. Reno, too, opposed the Vietnam War, but she had taken no part in the demonstrations. On election day in November 1972, McGovern suffered a crushing defeat at the hands of incumbent President Richard M. Nixon. Many of McGovern's Democratic followers—including Janet Reno—were also defeated.

It was a bitter disappointment for her.[3] She had expected positive results from her honest, dedicated work. Her thoughts turned to the advice once given her by former representative John B. Orr. In 1956, he had lost his seat in the Florida House of Representatives because of his speech declaring segregation to be morally wrong. "Janet, keep on doing and saying what you believe to be right," he said. "Don't pussyfoot, don't equivocate, don't talk out of both sides of your mouth, and you'll wake up the next morning feeling good about yourself."[4] Janet Reno had done and said what she believed to be right. That was some consolation.

There was little time to dwell on defeat. Soon after, in 1973, she was appointed as a special consultant to the Senate Criminal Justice Committee. In this position, Reno was responsible for the study and revision of Florida's criminal code. Her success in accomplishing this gained her, again, tremendous respect from many legislators, as well as from Governor Reubin Askew.

Later in 1973, Richard Gerstein, longtime Dade County state attorney, invited Reno to become a member of his staff. He did not know her, but her reputation of having an enormous capacity for work and great organizational skill, convinced him that he needed her. Reno agreed, but not readily, "I've always been a critic of yours," she insisted on telling him. She thought his prosecutors were more interested in securing convictions than in seeking justice. "You can come do something about that," he told her.[5]

Her assignment was to reorganize the state attorney's juvenile division. Regarding her work on this project, Seymour Gelber, administrative assistant to the state attorney in 1973, had this to say, "I thought she'd be lost in the morass and never emerge. Instead, weeks later, she tossed an outline on my desk for a whole new system."[6]

Once again Reno had won the respect of those who worked with her, and eventually she became administrative assistant to State Attorney Gerstein. During this period, Reno's desire for public service found a place in volunteer work for the community. From 1972 to 1974, she served as director of the YWCA of Greater Miami. In the following years, she served in the same capacity for the Children and Family Service Agency, and for the Children's Psychiatric Center. All of this provided invaluable experience in understanding community needs, and it gave the people a public servant who really cared and who offered solutions to their needs.

In 1976, Reno left the state attorney's office to accept an offer to join one of Florida's oldest and most prestigious firms, Steel, Hector, and Davis. In the same firm that had once denied her a summer job, Janet Reno now became their first woman partner.

Late in 1977, Richard Gerstein decided to retire from twenty-one years of service as state attorney. He sent Governor Reubin Askew two names to consider as a replacement for his unexpired term. One of those names was Janet Reno.

"I didn't need an awful lot of push on Janet," Governor Askew later recalled. "I had known and worked with her for many years. She is a person of tremendous integrity and professional competence. No one is going to intimidate Janet Reno."[7]

On January 3, 1978, the governor phoned Reno long-distance and asked her to be state attorney. She told him she would be honored.

The following day, Governor Askew flew from Tallahassee to Miami International Airport to meet the press. With her at his side, he announced Janet Reno as the new Dade County state attorney. She was the first woman to hold that position in the state of Florida.

The chief duties of a state (or district) attorney are to bring charges against and prosecute persons charged with a crime or offense. In criminal trials, he or she is the attorney for the people in that district. In some states, the state attorney is elected to office. In others, he or she is appointed. In this case, Reno was appointed to fill the unexpired term of the retiring state attorney. To keep this position, she would need to be elected by the voters the following November.

As state attorney of the Eleventh Judicial Circuit of Florida, Janet Reno had jurisdiction over the whole of Dade County, which is the Greater Miami area—including Coral Gables, Miami Beach, and Hialeah. Covering about ninety square miles, it had about 500,000 inhabitants, and was the largest city district in Florida.

Widespread publicity surrounded her appointment and the inaugural ceremony. If Janet Reno had not been known by the general public when she ran unsuccessfully for the legislature in 1972, she was certainly known now. And she set about immediately to prove she could do the job.

The new state attorney met first with Dade County Public Safety Director E. Wilson Purdy, to establish an understanding of their individual expectations. This had not been done before.

She rode along on patrol at least one night a week, with different police officers from different departments, to observe firsthand the difficulties of their work, and to learn how her office could assist them. To this end, she put the state attorney's office on twenty-four-hour call to any police officer who desired guidance at a crime scene.

To improve the quality of her staff, she recruited twenty new assistants with trial experience, both men

Janet Reno, appointed Florida's first woman state attorney by Governor Reubin Askew, is sworn in on January 4, 1978.

and women, and paid them salaries comparable to what they would earn in a large private law firm.

Reno assigned a top assistant to develop a domestic violence intervention program, whereby the state would prosecute any spouse who hurt his or her partner, unless the couple underwent counseling. This program was the first of its kind in the nation. Her aim was to curb violence in the home, which often leads to child abuse.

She learned to speak Spanish. In 1978, Dade County was more than one-third Latino. Not limiting herself to learning only courtesy words, Reno gave entire speeches in Spanish. She wanted to be state attorney to *all* the people.

This was only part of the action taking place during the early months of her appointment. "Miss Reno," as she was popularly called, also had to turn her energy toward campaigning for her election in November. If she could prove herself worthy as Dade County's chief prosecutor, the voters would respond favorably.

With only a limited personal budget, her campaign was truly conducted "on a shoestring." An advertising man was hired, but Reno wrote her own campaign brochure and speeches. The Reno ranch became campaign headquarters. Friends and family volunteered as her campaign staff. She refused any contributions with even the faintest conflict-of-interest possibility. She did her own public speaking. "Performance, Not Promises" was her campaign slogan.

When Janet Reno appeared before the voters, what did they see? A forty-year-old single woman, unusually tall, with a healthy outdoor look. Her shoulder-length hair was brushed into a simple, straight style. Her only cosmetic, a dash of lipstick, outlined a frequent, wide smile.

When she spoke, it was in a calm, firm voice to the voters.

> I make no promises except that I will try my best to make improvements in those areas of justice that are vital to the citizens of Dade.[8]
>
> My first priority is crimes of violence. A community is not worth living in if people don't feel safe in their homes and on the streets....
>
> Plea bargaining is a travesty. I shall continue to make a major effort to insure that justice is determined in an open courtroom and not by any deal made behind closed doors....
>
> We must prevent the encroachment of organized crime in this community. We must work with policy agencies to . . . apprehend and convict organized crime figures in Dade County....[9]

These and other issues, she presented to the public, usually ending with a brief family story, to put voters at ease about who she was.

On the cover of her campaign brochure, these words appeared: "Janet Reno was appointed State Attorney because she was the best person for the job. She still is."[10]

Apparently the voters of Dade County agreed. On election day in November 1978, Janet Reno was elected with 74 percent of the vote, even though she ran as a Democrat in a predominantly Republican county. Thus, she became the first woman in Florida's history to be elected as state attorney.

This was a tremendous victory for Janet Reno. There was great joy among her family, friends, and all those who believed in her. And now, she could and would work toward those improvements in justice that she considered so vital.

5

Making a Difference

Earlier in 1978, State Attorney Janet Reno had been the governor's choice. Now, this strong election victory had made her the people's choice. Many eyes would be watching her method of operation. The voters would soon find that their chief prosecutor was unafraid to make changes and promote new programs.

From her sixth-floor office in the Metro-Dade Justice Building, Reno supervised a staff of approximately ninety lawyers to prosecute the largest caseload of any district in the state of Florida. Their problems included street and domestic violence, felonies (murder, rape, burglary), drug abuse, illegal immigration, public corruption (bribery, dishonesty), among others. To keep abreast of this diversity, Reno recorded the lawyers and their assignments in a little black

Janet Reno as she appeared when she was Dade County state attorney.

notebook, which she carried with her. Thus, she could quickly check on who was handling a case and what progress had been made.

Among her priorities was the prevention of crime, not just punishment. From her work in the juvenile division in 1975, she understood the importance of a caring childhood to crime prevention.

Since Reno believed that children who see violence in their home often grow up to become angry and abusive themselves, she set up a child-support center. Here, children who had observed violence or had been a victim of violence, would talk with trained counselors in a relaxed, nonthreatening atmosphere. They could study their situation, and receive encouragement and guidance.

Another of her programs was enforcement of child support. Lawyers were assigned to pursue fathers who skipped out on making child-support payments. As state attorney, her demand to pay or be prosecuted brought results. She was the first Florida prosecutor ever to aggressively seek support. Annual collections almost doubled, and she won praise from women of every ethnic group. A rap artist, Luther Campbell, wrote a song in her honor: "Janet Reno comes to town, collecting all the money."[1]

In 1986, drug abuse became a major problem. Reno worked at getting local judges, police, and public defenders to establish a special drug court. This court sentenced nonviolent, first-time drug abusers to a year-long rehabilitation and education program. Thus, more prison space was made available for the really violent criminals, who needed to be locked up permanently, and it gave drug abusers a second chance to straighten out their lives.

The results were encouraging. More than half of those who completed the program appear to have remained drug-free. Because of its success, many cities around the nation have copied this idea.

Teenage violence has been a growing problem in almost every city. Here again, Reno came up with a risk-taking, new idea—wilderness camps. As an alternative to prison, some of Miami's most violent teenagers were sent off to camps. Here they learned discipline and were trained in a gainful occupation, which enabled them to develop self-esteem and to find a means to become self-supporting. The program showed a 50 percent success rate. This was higher than most other attempts to aid violent youth.

Although Janet Reno tried to be a fair prosecutor, she was not always seen that way by others. One of her most difficult challenges occurred early in her reign as state attorney. In 1980, her prosecutors failed to win the conviction of five police officers, who were charged with the beating death of a black insurance agent. The all-white jury's verdict set off three days of destructive rioting. The Liberty City section of Miami was torched. Enraged teens gutted and looted the first three floors of the Miami Justice Building. Angry residents blamed Reno. "Reno! Reno!" they shouted, marching through the streets. There were death threats. She couldn't sleep at home for nearly a month, and for safety, her widowed mother was moved to the home of relatives.

In the aftermath, Reno met tirelessly, day and night, with African-American citizens and leaders in an effort to reach an understanding. On hearing their concerns, she made many changes on issues important to minorities. Her office employed more African Americans and Latinos. To provide a more fair representation on juries, she signed a statement advocating that race not be a consideration when selecting a jury.

In time, African-American leaders praised her reforms. She appeared at many of their social and community affairs. As a member of the National Association for the Advancement of Colored People (NAACP), she began a personal tradition of marching every year in the Martin Luther King, Jr., Day parade. A prominent African-American attorney in Miami, H. T. Smith, recently said, "She does not allow race or sex to play any part in her hiring decisions, nor in her decisions to prosecute."[2] Once a sharp critic of Janet Reno, he is now one of her strongest supporters.

Janet Reno earned a reputation as a tough but fair prosecutor whose door was open to all. Although her workload grew, she continued to be the same informal, low-key person she had always been. One of her first acts

State Attorney Janet Reno meeting with a group of her prosecutors.

on moving into the state attorney's office was to personalize it. Not with framed diplomas and awards, but with photographs that represented her two passions—her family and the Florida outdoors. On display were photos of her father, her retired-attorney grandfather, her World War II pilot aunt, and a group photo of her family. On one wall hung a large photo of her mother, and Florida wildlife prints hung on the others.

She personalized relations with her staff as well, quickly learning the names of her ninety lawyers and many of their secretaries. Her staff was part of her family. She attended their birthday parties and family funerals. She urged new fathers to get home to their babies. She made sure that staff men and women had time to deal with family needs, and were allowed time off to attend their children's school programs. They frequently gathered at the Reno ranch for social occasions—barbecues, outdoor activities, and lively discussions on politics and law.

Despite Reno's informal style, she was taken very seriously by the staff. Among themselves, their boss was referred to as "JR" or "Her Tallness," but she was highly respected.[3] They knew, if pushed too far, she could flare up. Once she lost her patience with a group of judges, called them "dunderheads," and walked out of the room. Also, the staff had great respect for her "little black book"—the one in which she wrote down their assignments. The general feeling was that when she looked you up in the book, "you'd better have an answer."[4]

Reno's stamina was remarkable. She often arrived at her desk by 7:00 A.M., worked twelve hours, then rode with a police patrol or attended official functions at night.

The office cut into her social life, time with her family, and time to go exploring Florida waterways with her mother. Every four years there was another time-consuming campaign for reelection. Once her mother complained, "Politics! It eats up all your time . . . a public servant all the time, nights, and weekends." Reno patiently replied, "Mother, it was you who told me that politics has . . . the challenge of changing things for the better. I believed you, and I believe that's right."[5]

But politics alone did not "eat up" all of her time. Reno was soon to become a surrogate parent. A close friend, who was suffering a terminal illness, asked her to become legal guardian of her two children. Frances Webb and her late husband had been longtime friends of the Renos. When Frances died in November 1984, Reno became the guardian of Daphne and Daniel Webb, fifteen-year-old twins. She handled their finances, helped them with schoolwork, offered guidance, and included them in Reno family activities. They called her "Aunt Janny." She speaks of them warmly as her children.[6]

A pleasant part of Reno's official work was that of

speaking at the local schools. Staying in contact with children was important to her. She visited classrooms and talked to students about her duties as state attorney. She answered their questions, told them of her childhood, and gave them her home phone number to call if they were ever abused.

Reno believes that strong families are necessary for the prevention of crime. She would like every child to grow up in the way she and her sister and brothers did—with strong parenting, love, guidance, education, and a strong sense of right and wrong.[7]

In January 1988, she was invited to return to a school she had known well. At Coral Gables Senior High School, Janet Reno was inducted into the Hall of Fame, along with two other inductees, for outstanding achievement. In accepting this award, she told the Honor's Day assembly of one class in particular that had a lasting influence on her. "I learned from my physical education teacher the concept of competitive thought. She literally taught me how to win and lose."[8]

Every four years Janet campaigned, and each time the voters returned her to office. She had become one of the most widely respected public officials in Dade County. Meanwhile, Greater Miami had grown enormously in population, and so had the state attorney's office. Reno was now administering an office of 900 employees, including 230 attorneys, with a workload of more than 120,000 cases a year.

Election Day in November 1992 brought another victory to Reno, but the following month brought a grievous family loss. On December 21, her widowed mother died of lung cancer at the age of seventy-nine.

Jane Reno had been failing for some time, but this once vigorous woman, who loved to explore, wanted to keep going. "I don't want to be old and feeble," she said. And her four grown children agreed not to let her feel that way. Reno and various combinations of her sister, brothers, nieces, and nephews, escorted their aging matriarch across the country—west to California, north to Maine, south to the the Caribbean—to all the places she had always wanted to see. It was their gift to this woman who, even in death, celebrated the spirit of freedom. At her request, Jane Wood Reno's ashes were scattered over Biscayne Bay, to the reading of poetry chosen by her.[9]

Jane Reno's passing was a loss to a large band of admirers from South Florida, but the loss was especially felt by Janet Reno, who had always lived with her mother and shared her companionship. Little did she know that a new chapter in her life would soon be opening.

6

Answering the Call

On that day in November 1992 when Janet Reno was elected as state attorney for the fifth time, Bill Clinton, former governor of Arkansas, was elected President of the United States. One of President Clinton's first duties would be to appoint an official to head each of the thirteen departments that make up the President's Cabinet—the Department of Defense, Department of Agriculture, Department of Commerce, and so on.

Members of the Cabinet advise the president in making government decisions. One of the appointments to be made by President Clinton was that of U.S. attorney general, to head the Department of Justice.

Janet Reno's outstanding record as a prosecutor had been brought to the attention of the President by his brother-in-law Hugh Rodham, a public defender in the

Dade County Drug Court. Also, while campaigning in Florida for her husband's election, Hillary Rodham Clinton had met the Dade County state attorney and was favorably impressed. Soon after the President's election, administration officials contacted Reno to learn if she would consider a position in Washington. At that time, she was caring for her gravely ill mother and sent word that she could not leave Miami.

President Clinton interviewed several possible candidates, both men and women, to fill the post of attorney general. Having made a campaign promise to include more women in administrative positions, he submitted the name of corporate attorney Zoë Baird to the Senate Judiciary Committee as his nominee. She was forced to withdraw, however, when she was sharply criticized in connection with the employment of two illegal aliens as household help.[1] In the following weeks, the President seriously considered several other people to fill this important position. There was much speculation by the press as to who the nominee would be. U.S. District Court Judge Kimba Wood was believed to be a strong possibility, but she withdrew from consideration, in connection with employment of a domestic in her home.[2]

Early in February 1993, Janet Reno was summoned to the White House. No longer needed to care for her mother, she was now free to travel to Washington for a discussion with the President. It was reported that the two of them were in agreement on many important issues.

On February 11, 1993, President Clinton called for a press conference in the White House Rose Garden. There, a smiling chief executive introduced Janet Reno as his nominee for attorney general. He listed some of her many accomplishments in her fifteen years as Dade County's state attorney, and described her as "a frontline crime fighter and caring public servant, who truly had put the people first." After presenting several examples of her dedication to law and public service, the President ended his introduction of the attorney general nominee by saying, "Everyone I know who knows and has worked with Janet agrees that she possesses one quality most essential to being attorney general—unquestioned integrity. She's demonstrated throughout her career a commitment to principles that I want to see enshrined at the Justice Department: No one is above the law."[3]

In thanking the President, Reno said she was humbled by the honor given her, and would do her very best to deserve his confidence. She then outlined some of her goals, if she was confirmed. She would work toward the enforcement of civil rights laws, and seek stronger environmental laws. In keeping with her deep interest in the needs of children, she said:

> I would like to use the law of this land to do everything I possibly can to protect America's children from abuse and violence; to give to each

President Clinton held a press conference in the White House Rose Garden announcing Janet Reno as his nominee for attorney general on February 11, 1993.

of them the opportunity to grow, to be strong, healthy, and self-sufficient citizens of this country.[4]

Reno also stressed her desire to form a true partnership between local, state, and federal law enforcement agencies:

> I look forward to working with the President to build a Department of Justice that reflects a government of the people, by the people, for the people. A government in which people all across America come first.[5]

Questions from members of the press immediately followed, some addressed to the President, others to the nominee. Her manner was agreeable and relaxed. Her replies were clear and direct, leaving no doubt as to where she stood:

> *Question*: Can we get your views on the death penalty?
>
> *Reno*: I am personally opposed to the death penalty.

She then explained that although opposed to it, when the evidence and the law justify giving the death penalty, she will ask for it. She has asked for the death penalty in the past, and obtained it.

> *Question*: Are you a feminist?
>
> *Reno* (after a thoughtful pause): My mother always told me to do my best, to think my best, to do right, and consider myself a *person*.

Reno once told an interviewer, "I never characterized myself as a feminist. Who needed feminism when your Mom wrestled alligators?"[6] Friends say Reno has never worried about gender. "She has achieved success without any special consciousness of doing it as a woman. It seems natural to her to be doing it as a person."[7]

Question: Can you tell us your views on freedom of choice?

Reno: I am pro-choice.

(In 1973, in a case known as *Roe* v. *Wade,* the Supreme Court decided that women have a Constitutional right to choose to have an abortion. Those who agree with this decision are considered to be pro-choice. Those who disagree are considered to be pro-life.)

One of the final questions was addressed to President Clinton. "Mr. President, considering the long time it took to select a nominee, what would you have done differently?" His reply was instant. "I would have called Janet Reno on November the fifth!"[8] That was shortly after his election. And now, with the press conference ended, the President and Vice-President Al Gore escorted the attorney general nominee back into the White House.

Janet Reno's nomination drew praise from both Democrats and Republicans. The next step would be a thorough investigation of the nominee, including a background check by the FBI. The findings from this investigation would then be reviewed by the Senate Judiciary Committee, after which the official confirmation hearings would begin.

During this waiting period, good wishes were present wherever she went, but tension was present, too. The confirmation hearings, which lay ahead, could be grueling and the results uncertain.

The Senate Judiciary Committee consists of eighteen members, both Democrats and Republicans, who question the nominee to determine his or her qualifications and legal philosophy. After several days (sometimes weeks) of questioning, a committee vote is taken. From the results of this vote, the committee then recommends to the full Senate that the nominee either be confirmed or rejected. Or, the committee may choose to make no recommendation. Following this committee action, the full one-hundred-member Senate then votes to approve or reject the nomination.[9]

Janet Reno's confirmation hearing before the Senate Judiciary Committee was scheduled to begin on March 9, 1993. On that Tuesday morning, Reno was seated at a table in the center of Room 106 Dirksen in the Senate Office Building. Facing her were the seated committee members, a table and microphone before each member. It was an austere setting, one made particularly eerie by the lighting from television cameras placed around the room.

The U.S. Capitol building, in which the Senate Judiciary confirmation hearings for Janet Reno took place.

Senator Joseph R. Biden, Jr., a Democrat from Delaware, presided as chairperson. "You have no idea how happy we are to see you here," he said in his opening remarks. Then he explained that if confirmed, she would be the first attorney general with a "broad, deep, extensive background in criminal justice issues."[10]

In her opening statement, Reno said she was honored to be with them, and then spoke of her childhood and her parents' influence on her life. She told of her father coming from Denmark at the age of twelve, and being teased about his clothes and his accent. Later, when he became a police reporter for the *Miami Herald* and had to report on bad happenings in the community, he was always fair—never mean. "I think he remembered what it was like to be teased."[11]

Reno told of the family's need for a bigger house, and not having much money, of her mother's determination to build one—digging the foundation with a pick and shovel, and laying the blocks with her own hands. "I have lived in that house ever since," said Reno. She recalled Hurricane Andrew striking in August 1992, and how her frail mother sat inside totally unafraid—knowing how she had built that house. "She hadn't compromised her standards. She had built it the right way."[12] And it survived.

Reno spoke briefly about her fifteen years as Florida's chief prosecutor, and of what the state attorney's office had accomplished in dealing with violent crime, career criminals, and drugs. In closing, she quoted an inscription on the Department of Justice building: "Justice in the life and conduct of the state is possible only as it first resides in the heart and souls of the citizens." Referring to the many citizens who believe in and yearn for justice, Reno said, "I want to do everything I can, if you confirm me, to work with them as their lawyer to seek justice."[13]

Now it was time for questions from the Senate committee. Each senator is allowed thirty minutes for direct questioning. After the entire eighteen members have participated, each is allowed another thirty minutes.

Reno welcomed their questions, and answered each in her characteristic calm, firm, thoughtful manner. Most of the topics focused on her experience in fighting crime, and her plans for dealing with it. She cited her belief in combining tough punishment for criminals, with opportunities for rehabilitation in cases in which that might be appropriate. She also stressed the need for early intervention education to draw children away from an acceptance of violence. Other topics covered were her views on handgun control, immigration, terrorism, and the death penalty, among other things.

Throughout the hearings, Reno's self-confidence and understanding of difficult issues seemed to be reassuring to the committee. So reassuring that after only the second full day of questioning, the members voted immediately and unanimously for confirmation of her appointment.

The following day, the committee's recommendation was sent to the Senate. Here, although only a majority vote was needed, the full Senate confirmed the appointment of Janet Reno in a rare 98–0 vote. When the results were announced, the normally proper Senate chamber was filled with applause. Senator Robert "Bob" Graham, former Democratic governor of Florida and a fellow Harvard graduate, said, "I have never been prouder to be a citizen of Florida than I have been these last several days with Janet."[14] He had been one of Reno's advisors in preparing for the hearings.

The swearing-in ceremony took place the next morning, March 12, 1993, in the Roosevelt Room of the White House. A distinguished crowd had assembled to witness this unprecedented occasion—Vice-President Gore, Senate and House Judiciary Committee members, others from Congress, special friends, and of course, Reno's large, enthusiastic family, including her new grandniece.

In his welcome message, President Clinton praised Reno for her qualities of leadership and integrity, for sharing the stories of her family and career during the confirmation hearings, and for her work in public service:

> As Janet Reno begins her work at the Justice Department, she will enter a building that

Janet Reno being sworn into office by Supreme Court Justice Byron R. White, as President Clinton witnesses the ceremony. Holding the Bible is Reno's niece, who is also named Janet Reno.

symbolizes our nation's commitment to justice, to equality, to the enforcement of our laws. On the side of that building . . . is the inscription, 'The halls of justice are a hallowed place.' With Janet Reno serving as our nation's attorney general, those words will have great meaning for all Americans.[15]

And then, with the President by her side and her fourteen-year-old niece, also named Janet, holding the Bible, the official ceremony began. Her right hand raised, and her left on the Bible, Janet Reno was sworn into office by Supreme Court Justice Byron R. White.

After the hearty applause which followed, the new attorney general acknowledged with thanks the honor she had been given. She spoke of having sensed that there will be:

> . . .a new spirit in America where people will want to become involved in public service, because it is the greatest undertaking you can commit for your nation. . . . This is a new and wonderful time in American history, where we want to make government reflective of its people, make its people come first, and give all Americans an opportunity to be attorney general, senators, and serve the people.[16]

And now, fifty-four-year-old Janet Reno had become the nation's seventy-eighth attorney general, and the first woman in history to hold that office. She had been called upon to bring her collective experience to the top law enforcement office in the United States.

7

A Full Agenda

As chief legal officer of the entire nation, Attorney General Reno was well aware of the magnitude of her new position.

The first attorney general had been appointed in 1789 by President George Washington. As a member of the Cabinet, he gave legal advice to the President and argued cases before the Supreme Court. As the nation grew, the number of legal problems increased. On June 22, 1870, Congress established the Department of Justice, with the attorney general as head of the department. The duties of this office include direction and control over U.S. attorneys and all other counsel employed on behalf of the United States, and also supervisory power over U.S. marshals, clerks, and other officers of the federal courts. In addition, the attorney general provides legal advice to the President, reviews suggestions for filling positions of federal judges, U.S. attorneys, and U.S. marshals, and makes recommendations to the President concerning these appointments.[1]

Today, there are ninety-three U.S. attorneys stationed throughout the United States, Puerto Rico, the Virgin Islands, Guam, and the Northern Marianas (an island group near the Philippines, administered by the United States). They are appointed by the President and confirmed by the Senate for a term of four years, or at the discretion of the President. They and their assistant U.S. attorneys are responsible for handling most of the criminal and civil lawsuits for the United States. The attorney general is responsible for the conduct of these legal proceedings.[2]

The Justice Department has been described as the largest law office in the world. It employs approximately 92,300 people throughout the world, who perform various law enforcement functions. This is a marked contrast to the staff of nine hundred that Janet Reno had previously supervised as Florida's state attorney. But she had known most of her staff in Dade County, and she was not about to lose her personal touch.

Shortly after settling into her new post, Reno invited the Justice Department employees to a meeting in the building's courtyard. Here, she introduced herself as "the new kid on the block," explaining that she wanted them to know "my hopes and dreams and how I do things."[3] She said that, while she was attorney general, each problem to be handled would be addressed with one question: "What's the right thing to do?" Admitting that the answer is not always clear, she encouraged her staff to debate with her on disagreements, because debate can sometimes lead to an understanding of what to do.

And what were her hopes and dreams? On this particular day, she listed only a few:

- Restore the image of the Justice Department as a place of truth and justice. She cautioned her prosecutors to explain their actions in words everyone can understand. "Too often, lawyers have made the law a mystery. We must make it a lamp that shines the way."[4]

- Urge Congress to repeal the mandatory minimum sentences for drug-related crimes, and assign nonviolent addicts to treatment programs. As often before, she spoke on the need for using our prison space for the really violent criminals.

- Toughen the enforcement of existing environmental laws.

- Reform courts in a way that would give ordinary people greater access to justice. She believes that the courts, lawyers, and the Department of Justice are not always there for the average American.

Among those who listened, there could be little doubt that their new attorney general had a clear vision of ways to improve our system of justice. But first, she must deal with several grave problems that had been present when she took office.

One of these problems involved a religious cult known as the Branch Davidians. Its members had amassed an arsenal of weapons on a seventy-eight-acre compound near the town of Waco, Texas. On February 28, agents from the Bureau of Alcohol, Tobacco, and Firearms (ATF) went to the compound to serve an arrest warrant for illegal possession of firearms. This turned into a gun battle in which four federal agents were killed and sixteen wounded. Six Davidians were believed to have also died in the battle. A standoff resulted, and the FBI from the Department of Justice was called in to handle the problem.

Cult leader David Koresh, a charismatic psychopath, had convinced his followers that he was the Messiah. As such, he forced his will upon them. Reports from former cult members indicated that not only had an arsenal been accumulated, but there was sexual abuse of women and children, with cruel punishment inflicted on the disobedient.[5]

After the shoot-out, twenty-one youngsters, age five months to twelve years, were released to the custody of the Texas child-welfare agency, and were taken to the Methodist Home for Children. Their conversations with therapists indicated the presence of child abuse, beatings, and rape inside the compound.[6]

Over the seven tense weeks of futile negotiation that followed, Koresh became increasingly menacing. There was growing fear of ongoing child abuse and other forms of torment to those who were barricaded inside.

In April, FBI Director William Sessions and his top deputies presented a plan of action to Attorney General Reno. Not receptive to the plan, she called for further study and investigation. The plan was to break through a wall and pump nonlethal tear gas into the compound, which would cause Koresh and his followers to come out and be willing to negotiate.[7]

Janet Reno was not convinced. She asked hundreds of questions. Army officials were consulted for their past hostage experience. Top professional experts with experience in dealing with paranoid cult figures were consulted. When Reno continued to press about the dangers of tear gas, a leading toxicologist assured her that the gas was not permanently harmful, nor carcinogenic, nor would it cause future birth defects.[8]

After exhaustively studying the situation from every angle, and being ever-aware of the children, it was strongly felt, were held hostage by an alleged madman, the attorney general reluctantly reached a decision. She discussed it with President Clinton, and then gave her approval of the plan.

Early on the morning of April 19, after a fifty-one

day standoff, FBI agents called out over loudspeakers, one last time, for Koresh and his followers to surrender peacefully. When no response was made, an armored vehicle broke through a wall of the building, and tear gas was pumped in. When fired upon, the vehicle backed off—waiting for the people to come out. But in the silence that followed, no one came out.

Suddenly, a massive explosion rocked the building. The arsenal of ammunition had blown up. Then a blazing fire erupted and destroyed everything inside, including the people—adults and children.[9] In the investigation that followed, it was learned that cult members had started the fires that ignited the arsenal. Koresh and several of his followers had died from gunshot wounds, although none of the federal agents had fired a shot. In all, eighty-six cult members, including seventeen children, perished in the flames.[10]

The nation watched in horror as television news cameras recorded the tragedy. But no one was more deeply affected than Attorney General Reno, who had made the final decision. That afternoon, she went before television cameras in a special news report to explain the disaster at Waco. Solemn-faced and obviously anguished, she told the nation that it was she, not the FBI, not the White House, who would answer for the tragedy. "I approved the plan and I'm responsible for it. The buck stops with me."[11]

That evening, she willingly appeared on CNN's

Larry King Live. For one hour she explained in detail the events leading up to her decision, and answered call-in questions from viewers throughout the country. One question Larry King asked was, "Was this the toughest day of your career?" Janet Reno replied, "It's certainly one of the toughest, and certainly one of the very most painful and saddest."[12]

It was painful and sad to all who watched. But in her honesty, visible anguish, and courage under enormous pressure, Janet Reno had won the respect of many. This became quite evident on April 28, following the House Judiciary Committee hearing on the Waco tragedy.

Reno had testified for more than three hours, and had continued to take responsibility for the decision to use tear gas. Most of the committee understood her action and praised her conduct. One representative, however, called the operation a "profound disgrace," and then said, "I'd like you to know that there is at least one member of Congress that isn't going to rationalize the death of two dozen children."

In a clear but shaking voice, Reno replied, "I haven't tried to rationalize the deaths of children, Congressman. I feel more strongly about it than you will *ever* know. But I have neither tried to rationalize the deaths of four ATF agents. . . . Most of all, Congressman, I will not engage in recrimination."[13]

At the end of that long session before the Judiciary Committee, Reno returned to her office at the Justice

Attorney General Janet Reno is interviewed on CNN's *Larry King Live*, following the Waco tragedy on April 19, 1993.

Department. There, her staff, who had been following the hearing, gave her a standing ovation.[14] Yes, she had won the respect of many.

The following October, a Justice Department investigative report concluded that Janet Reno had exhausted all "reasonable alternatives" before approving the assault on David Koresh's Waco compound in April. It cleared the attorney general of having made any mistakes.[15]

Another shocking event, which occurred prior to her appointment and needed careful consideration, was the World Trade Center bombing. On February 26, a massive explosion rocked the twin towers of Manhattan's World Trade Center, killing six people and injuring over one thousand. The cause was found to be a van filled with explosives that had been left in the underground parking garage.

Believing the explosion to be the work of terrorists, the FBI and other intelligence agencies swiftly mobilized to locate those responsible. A ring of suspected terrorists was arrested, charged with conspiracy to carry out the bombing, and held without bail. Sheik Omar Abdel Rahman, the Egyptian spiritual leader of a Muslim fundamentalist group, was suspected of masterminding the bomb plot, but he was not arrested.

Day after day, Reno was urged by people within the government, the press, and the nation to arrest the sheik before he could leave the country. Although she had him under constant surveillance, Reno felt the legal evidence was not sufficient to arrest him. But early in July, while being tracked by FBI agents, he tried to flee; she ordered Immigration and Naturalization Service (INS) agents to arrest him. His arrest was legally justified now because of a case pending against him by the INS. While a case is pending, the defendant is forbidden to leave the United States. Now, with all the suspects imprisoned to await the upcoming terrorist trial, the pressure on the attorney general about this matter was lessened.

Meanwhile, other matters required her attention. Many complaints were being filed by disabled rights groups against small businesses and municipalities. Congress passed the Americans with Disabilities Act in 1991. It requires that businesses and other public areas be made accessible to people with physical disabilities. Two years later, many small businesses and municipalities had not complied with this federal law. In response to the complaints, Reno announced that enough time had been allowed to make the necessary changes, and those not in compliance would be taken to court.

Other complaints were being filed about racial bias among lenders in making home loans. The Fair Housing Act of 1968 and subsequent legislation make it illegal to discriminate against people seeking public housing or mortgage loans. But 1992 figures drawn from reports by home-mortgage lenders showed that, with comparable

Attorney General Reno, in her conference room, meeting with a disability rights group.

income levels, African-American and Hispanic applicants were denied home loans more often than white applicants.[16] Attorney General Reno, along with Housing and Urban Development (HUD) Secretary Henry G. Cisneros, attended a Senate Banking Committee hearing on this matter in November 1993. They pledged tougher enforcement of fair-lending laws. That is, laws that bar discrimination in granting mortgage loans, home equity loans, and the refinancing of existing mortgages.

Another matter of concern to the attorney general, as well as the INS, is the flood of illegal immigrants entering the United States. Arriving without documents or with fraudulent documents, they come seeking political asylum. Each one must go through a hearing process before being approved or denied admission. With 85,000 requests yearly, the processing facilities are overloaded. In addition, many illegal aliens cross our southern borders undetected. Reno has announced a plan to increase the number of U.S. Border Patrol officers to more than one thousand, mainly in California and Texas. It also calls for an increased use of technology for tracking and deterring illegal immigrants from crossing the border.[17]

Adding to the immigration problem in 1994, thousands of Cubans were fleeing economic poverty in their Communist homeland. Risking their lives on makeshift rafts and boats, they traveled ninety miles across the treacherous Straits of Florida to reach the Florida coast. This deluge of refugees caused the Clinton administration to reverse a twenty-eight year policy of granting asylum to Cubans. On September 9, 1994, an agreement was reached in which the United States would accept at least 20,000 legal Cuban immigrants each year, and Fidel Castro would stop his citizens from fleeing.

During the past few years, violence aimed at abortion clinics has become a widespread problem. Dozens of clinics nationwide have been the target of blockades, bombings, and arson by antiabortion activists. In March 1993, a Florida doctor, who was an abortion provider, was shot to death near his clinic by an antiabortion activist. Janet Reno called it "a horrible crime," and told reporters she would do everything she could to pursue an appropriate federal response.[18]

Two months later, she appeared at a hearing on a bill, drafted by Massachusetts Senator Edward M. Kennedy, to which she gave strong support. The bill, passed by Congress in November 1993, is known as the Freedom of Access to Clinic Entrances Act. This act makes it a federal crime to obstruct access to abortion clinics, destroy their property, injure their workers, or intimidate their patients. The act does, however, allow peaceful protests. Signed by President Clinton on May 27, 1994, it became law, effective immediately.[19]

One of the earlier problems inherited by Janet Reno when she became attorney general, was that of FBI

Vice President Al Gore and Attorney General Janet Reno answering questions at a Town Hall Meeting.

leadership. In January, a lengthy report had been issued by the Justice Department's Office of Professional Responsibility, charging FBI Director William S. Sessions with abusing the privileges of his office. President Clinton asked the new attorney general to review the case, and advise him on whether to seek Sessions' resignation.

Once again Reno was questioned repeatedly by news reporters and others about the investigation, and about the probable fate of the FBI chief. But she would not be rushed into judgment. Her recommendation to the President, she assured them, would be based on a "fair objective judgment."

In July, after a thorough investigation of all the facts, Reno advised the President that the charges were justified. Sessions was asked to resign. When he refused, the President was forced to dismiss him.[20]

The following day, July 20, 1993, President Clinton nominated Louis J. Freeh as the new FBI director. A former FBI agent, U.S. attorney, and present U.S. district court judge, Freeh was heralded as the most prepared for this post of any FBI director in history. Both Democrats and Republicans praised the nomination, and his impressive credentials led the way for an early confirmation by Congress.

By this time, Janet Reno had been deeply immersed for several months in making weighty decisions that affected people throughout the entire nation. But she

The FBI Building in Washington, D.C., is home of the Federal Bureau of Investigation, America's criminal investigation system.

continued to be the same unpretentious person as before. Her naturalness came through at unexpected moments.

The formal swearing-in ceremony for the new FBI chief took place on September 1, 1993. It began with the attorney general presenting President Clinton to the assembled dignitaries, the family and friends of Judge Louis J. Freeh, and invited guests. In her opening remarks Reno said, "The first job I ever had was at the Metro-Dade Sheriff's Department. I never thought that I would stand here and introduce the President of the United States as the next Director of the FBI was sworn in."[21]

It was a confession of awe and respect that many who were listening could understand.

8

Curbing Violence

Over the years the problem of violent crime in America had been steadily growing. By 1993 an epidemic of violence had swept across the nation. Grim tales of death by random killers were reported almost daily on television and in newspaper headlines: "Gunman opens fire in parking lot, killing two;" "Seven slain in fast food restaurant;" "Six gunned down on Long Island train."

Of the several types of violent crime—fistfighting, shooting, stabbing, rape, robbery, assault—shooting appears to be the number one choice. Too often, gun-killing has become the way to settle an argument or a grudge. Every fourteen minutes someone in America dies from a gunshot wound.[1]

This violence is not limited to adults. At a town meeting discussion, President Clinton remarked that teen violence may be the biggest problem we have in urban America. Attorney General Reno agreed, when she spoke at Harvard University. "I think youth violence is the single greatest crime problem in America today."[2]

As the death toll rises, what can be done to stop these outrageous acts of violence?

Appearing on ABC's television news program *Nightline*, to discuss "Gun Violence Against Kids," the attorney general clearly expressed her views:

> I think the first thing you do is try to get guns off the streets, by making sure that only people who know how to safely and lawfully use them, and demonstrate that ability, can be licensed to use them. . . . I think you get guns off the streets as much as possible. I think another thing you do is let children understand that they don't settle disputes with guns.[3]

Congress took a first step in getting guns off the street when it passed the Brady bill into law in November 1993. This law imposes a nationwide waiting period for the purchase of handguns. It requires a waiting period of five business days, while local police conduct a criminal background check on prospective handgun buyers. Among those ineligible to buy a handgun are convicted felons, fugitives, minors, drug and alcohol addicts, and illegal immigrants.[4]

The Brady law is named after former White House press secretary James S. Brady. In 1981, Brady was severely wounded and permanently disabled in an assassination attempt on President Ronald Reagan. Brady and his wife, Sarah, along with other gun-control advocates fought nearly seven years for this legislation. It had been strongly opposed by the National Rifle Association and its congressional allies.

Opposition to gun control is based in part on the Second Amendment of the United States Constitution which states:

> A well-regulated militia, being necessary to the security of a free State, the right of the people to keep and bear arms, shall not be infringed.[5]

On the frontier, a rifle or shotgun was usually a pioneer family's only protection against wild animals and prowling enemies. In today's society, the right to bear arms has often been interpreted as the right to bear not only rifles and shotguns, but also handguns and assault weapons.

The Brady law is the first major antigun legislation in the country since 1968. Jim Brady has said that if this law had been in effect in 1981, the deranged young man who shot down the President, a Secret Service agent, a Washington police officer, and Brady himself, would never have been permitted to buy the handgun he used.[6]

Along with the growing fear of violence, there also has been a growing distaste for the violence seen on television. In some homes the television is on from morning until night. Great numbers of children, from infancy on, are exposed to a constant outpouring of graphic violence—beatings, rapes, murders. Parents, educators, and child psychologists fear that this antisocial behavior may negatively affect young viewers. Since children often imitate what they see, several have already been injured, and even lost their lives imitating scenes from a television program or a movie.

Early in October, a television cartoon was blamed when a five-year-old boy in Ohio set fire to a mobile home that killed his baby sister. He had watched MTV's *Beavis and Butthead* in which the characters lit fires for fun. Expressing regret over the tragedy, MTV programmers immediately deleted all references to fire in future *Beavis and Butthead* episodes and moved the cartoon to a later time slot.[7]

The Senate Commerce Committee began hearings in October 1993 on possible legislation aimed at curbing violence on television. Attorney General Reno was among the witnesses, along with representatives from the movie and television industry, the National PTA (Parent-Teacher Association), and other citizens wanting a government response to the problem. One panel of citizens told the senators they had been coming to these meetings for many years to no avail. They wanted to see some legislative action.

In her testimony, Reno urged the television industry

to make significant reductions in violent programming during the coming year. She told them:

> All I am asking today is that the entertainment industry—and that includes the movies, the broadcasting networks, cable TV, and the independents—acknowledge their role and their responsibilities, and pledge to work with us to use every tool they have to address the problem. And more than pledging, start doing something about it now.

She cautioned, also, that if voluntary steps are not taken soon, "the federal government may have to take action."[8]

Her remarks brought a mixture of protest and denial from the industry. However, a "TV Violence Report Card," released by North Dakota's Senator Byron L. Dorgan, shows that children witness an average of seventy-six acts of violence per hour on Saturday morning cartoons.[9] According to the National Coalition on TV Violence, violence is defined as "the deliberate and hostile use of overt force by one individual against another."[10]

Three bills aimed at protecting young viewers are under consideration by the Senate Commerce Committee. One would prohibit violent programming during hours when children are most likely to watch television. Another requires warnings before and during violent programs. A third bill calls on the FCC (Federal

Communication Commission) to survey television programming four times a year, and to list the most violent programs and their sponsors.[11]

The passage of these bills could be another positive step in the government's effort to curb violence. But the attorney general also emphasizes the role of parents in this effort. "It's parents' responsibility to make sure they know what their children are doing."[12] *The New York Times* columnist Anna Quindlen agrees. This mother of three young children writes, "Parents, not TV, must be responsible for their children. . . . Making the distinction between what they want to do and what is good for them—that's a parent's job description."[13]

A major plan to fight crime and violence was presented to Congress by the President in the fall of 1993. Known as the anticrime bill, many of its provisions can be recognized as those favored also by the attorney general. Some of the highlights of the anticrime bill are:

Boot Camps. The bill provides for military-style boot camps, where first-time offenders will be given the discipline, the education, and the training needed to avoid a lifetime of crime.

Increase in Police Officers. A five-year program to put up to 50,000 new police officers on neighborhood streets to "walk the beat." The program would create a Police Corps to pay for the schooling of youths who become police officers.

Death Penalty. The federal death penalty would be expanded to include some fifty federal crimes, such as the murder of a federal judge or law enforcement officer, and killings by terrorists and carjackers. It would also limit the time available for death-row inmates to appeal their sentences.

Mandatory Drug Treatment. Drug treatment would be given to inmates in federal and state prisons.

Gun Control. Tighter licensing rules for gun dealers would go into effect, as well as a ban on handgun sales to youths under eighteen, and a ban on assault weapons.[14]

Attorney General Reno was particularly pleased with the proposed ban on assault weapons. The Department of Defense defines an assault weapon as a military rifle, capable of firing fully automatic—that is, firing all the cartridges, stored in a firearm, with only one pull of the trigger.[15]

"An assault weapon's only purpose is to kill people," said Janet Reno on NBC's program *Meet the Press*. "We need to clearly distinguish between assault weapons and guns used for sporting purposes. Weapons that are used solely for the purpose of killing someone don't belong on our streets."[16]

Two states—New Jersey and California—have already outlawed assault weapons within their borders.[17]

This anticrime bill is the largest in history. It was created in response to public demand for government

Attorney General Janet Reno addressing a meeting of the United States Sentencing Commission.

action to curb the spread of crime. Its measures were studied and debated and refined in both the House and Senate before finally being approved, after which it was sent on to the President. Among the refinements, the bill provided for hiring 100,000 new police officers instead of 50,000. Also, it provided for building more prisons, and for creating community programs to prevent crime. On September 13, 1994, signed by President Clinton, this bill became the Crime Law.

Of the many steps being taken to control crime and violence, Reno believes that attacking the root cause of crime could be the most effective. And that starts with children and family. "Government agencies must concentrate on preventing social problems rather than treating their effects," says the attorney general.[18]

Behavior experts indicate that the years from birth to three of a child's life are crucial to his or her future behavior. It is in these years that a child learns right from wrong, and the concept of reward and punishment. "What difference does it make what punishment we provide at 18, 19, and 20," says Reno, "if children haven't developed the concept of punishment in the early formative years?"[19]

At a Women's Bar Association of Washington dinner, the attorney general presented her national agenda for children. Beginning with a nationwide effort to prevent teen pregnancy, it includes prenatal care for every pregnant woman in the United States; education and preventive medicine for toddlers; intervention in families where child abuse, neglect, or learning problems exist; truancy prevention; and a summer job program that teaches teenagers marketable skills.[20]

Clearly, Attorney General Janet Reno feels strongly that improving conditions for America's children is vital to the nation's law enforcement program.

9

Her Two Worlds

We have looked at Janet Reno as the attorney general—her heavy responsibilities, the difficult decisions she must make that are not always popular. But what about Janet Reno the person? How has her life changed since becoming America's top law enforcement officer?

The first change was her move to Washington, D.C., where she rented a small, one-bedroom apartment. Completely furnished, including coffeepot, ironing board, and television, this would be adequate for her simple needs. "I'm not a good housekeeper," she says.[1]

Located only a few blocks from the Justice Department, she planned to walk to work. And she did. The day after being sworn in, Reno trudged through a swirling blizzard, wearing an old sweater and Everglades boots—her security agents close behind.

The new attorney general's lack of pretension became even more clear when her legal staff and others—including David Brinkley on ABC News *This Week*—asked how to address her. "Do you want to be called General?" Her reply was decisive. "Don't call me General. I don't think Generals belong in the law. Ms. Reno or Janet or Hey you is fine."[2]

Like other Department of Justice employees, her working day begins when she puts on her ID badge and shuttles through metal detectors at the building entrance. Arriving at her fifth-floor office about 7:00 A.M., Reno first goes through the current stack of correspondence. An hour later, she meets with her staff, going over the day's agenda and listing it on a yellow legal pad. At 9:00 A.M. her schedule of appointments begins, often continuing nonstop until 10:00 P.M. or later.

During an interview at Harvard Law School in the spring of 1993, Reno spoke of her agenda for one particular day. The morning began in her conference room, where she met with a group of incoming U.S. attorneys. Then, it was off to a local elementary school located in a neighborhood troubled by drive-by shootings. Here, she addressed community leaders and several classes of students about their safety concerns. At the White House Rose Garden, she joined the President

Janet Reno welcomed the Rainbow Crusaders from Florida, to the Department of Justice. The group delivers its anti-drug message to audiences across the country.

for a press conference announcing a proposed increase in police officers on the streets. Returning to the Justice Department, Reno met with a candidate for assistant attorney general. Later, she spoke with reporters from the *American Bar Association Journal*, and much later, joined some college friends for dinner before returning to her apartment.[3] Is it any wonder that when asked in a survey of "What top lawyers are reading," her reply was, "Who has time to read?" But she does keep books of poetry at her bedside. Some of her favorite poets are Samuel Taylor Coleridge, Rudyard Kipling, and Maya Angelou.

With her tight schedule, Reno tries to maintain a simple lifestyle. Lunching in the basement cafeteria of the Justice Department, she grabs a tray, joins the line—greeting those nearby—and selects her meal. She pays at the register, even when told on her first day, "Compliments of the manager." "Oh no, I have to pay," says Reno.[4] And she does. Seating herself at whatever table is available appears to surprise other workers. Former attorney generals have been more aloof. This one wants to remain accessible.

That's not always easy when security demands she be accompanied by the FBI. Reno likes to ride the Metro—Washington's subway and bus system—much to the dismay of her security agents. How can a six-foot-one woman blend in? Far less conspicuous is the dark-blue Lincoln used for her official transportation, the driver an FBI agent. But her independent nature is not easily suppressed. Soon after becoming attorney general, when planning a quick trip to Miami, she insisted on flying commercial so she could pay for the trip herself. "But what about your security?" reporters asked. "I don't know," she said, with a hint of impatience. "I just know I'm going home and I'm paying for it!"[5]

Janet Reno has always been known for paying her own way. She buys her cars at the sticker price instead of asking for a better deal. She spurns any offer of free parking or other special privileges, explaining, "I'm in public office, I'm a public servant, I don't take favors."[6]

With constant demands on her time, how does Reno maintain a balance between her professional and personal life? As state attorney in Dade County, she could leave the office at night for the wooded haven of the Reno ranch. But living in a city apartment, ever under the public eye, and on call for any internal crisis in the nation's security, how does she work off stress? For a woman who mowed her own lawn and chain-sawed trees for firewood, her sister and brothers have laughingly suggested they might plant holly trees on the apartment building roof, so she could have some wood to saw.

With little time for the fitness workouts of many health-conscious Americans, Reno fits in her own form of exercise whenever she can. "I try to walk each morning between 6:00 and 7:00, and explore a new part

Janet Reno spoke at the installation of Patricia A. Seitz (center), first woman president of the Florida State Bar Association. Appearing with them is Florida Chief Justice Rosemary Barkett (right).

of Washington," she says. "Weekends I am trying to take longer walks, and Saturday afternoons I look forward to going to museums or other points of interest in the city."[7] In the summer, with the Potomac River nearby, she looks forward to canoeing and also hiking in the mountains.

Often when walking on the Mall, past the Smithsonian's National Museum of Natural History, Reno is reminded of her mother. Only a short time ago, she wheeled her seventy-nine-year-old parent through the Museum to view the dinosaur skeletons. Her mother's vision was failing along with her battle with lung cancer, but she could still see large things—and she loved dinosaurs, Reno recalls. Jane Wood Reno was known to be sharply outspoken, and sometimes outrageous, but her daughter remembers her warmly. "She was my best friend," Reno says.[8]

As the end of December approached during the attorney general's first year in Washington, she was asked by the press what she would be doing over the holidays. She replied that she would be going home to spend Christmas with her family. Home to Janet Reno is still the house her mother built. Over the years, the original twenty-one acres has been reduced to a comfortable three and one-half. From time to time, parcels of land had been sold off to finance major events—college tuition for the Reno children; travel for Jane to Australia, the Galapagos Islands, and Greece. It is to this house, the Reno ranch, that Janet returns for the holidays and special family gatherings.

Does her family treat her differently now that she has the distinctive title of Attorney General of the United States? Not really. She is still Janny to them. Robert, Maggy, Mark, and their sister get together in good spirits as they always have, recalling family tales and adding some of their own. Like their sister Janet, they all are engaged in interesting work. Robert is a columnist for *New York Newsday*, Maggy Hurchalla serves as a county commissioner in central Florida, and Mark is a sea captain.

As time passes, Reno's family keeps expanding with nieces, nephews, their spouses, and a recent grandniece. Also, of course, there are "her children," Daphne and Daniel Webb—now grown and pursuing their own careers.

Friends say Reno's one regret is that she never married and had children. They talk of young suitors earlier in her life. Reno says she wanted to get married and have lots of children, but never could find the right person. "What I wanted . . . and I think my mother was the one that described this to us as we were growing up: 'Don't marry anybody unless, when you're around them, your heart goes potato-potato-potato, and your mind thinks that it's the right thing to do.'"[9]

But Reno has many friends and is a friend to great numbers of children. Wherever she is on a speaking

Janet Reno enjoys visiting with children. Here she is signing autographs for the schoolchildren at River Terrace Community School in Washington, D.C.

engagement, she tries also to speak to the schoolchildren in that area. When groups of schoolchildren come to see her, she greets them with a smile and welcomes them into her Justice Department conference room—a panelled, high-ceiling room, with a colorful mural above the fireplace. Inviting her visitors to ask questions, she assures them that students ask better questions than reporters. No matter how hectic the office may be—phones jangling and people needing attention—Reno remains totally involved with them. She is their friend, and they sense it.

The reactions of her young visitors are honest and often refreshing. After Lani Guinier, law professor at the University of Pennsylvania, introduced her six-year-old son to the towering attorney general, he reported that he would tell his classmates "he had met the federal government."[10]

Earlier, Lani Guinier had been considered by President Clinton to head the Civil Rights Division of the Justice Department. When her arguments in several law review articles were attacked as too radical, he withdrew her nomination. Reno, however, had continued to back her nomination, saying she found the articles "thought-provoking."[11]

Now in her fifties, stately tall, with an auburn glint in her short layered hair, and the same generous smile, Janet Reno is one of the most admired women in America. In Washington, her office is deluged with calls and letters from well-wishers and requests for interviews; she is also in demand as a speaker. People admire her straight-forward manner, her courage and common sense. *The New York Times* calls her "a prized asset."[12] In the most-admired-woman poll of *Good Housekeeping* readers, Janet Reno ranks among such luminaries as Mother Teresa, former First Lady Barbara Bush, and current First Lady Hillary Rodham Clinton.[13]

Followed by camera crews and pursued by reporters and autograph collectors, she doggedly focuses on the more serious business at hand. Her fame stems from that day on April 19, when she appeared on CNN News and sadly but unflinchingly accepted responsibility for the Waco disaster. "The buck stops with me"[14] was the kind of straight-talk that Americans could appreciate.

Newsweek calls her "The Reluctant Star," and asks how she deals with all this attention. "I'm a person just like anyone else," she says. "I can't let it go to my head. I just try to figure out what the right thing is, then try to do it."[15]

For Janet Reno, one of the "right things" she does is reach out to young adults and share with them her values and her vision for America. In a 1993 commencement address at Barry University in Miami, she spoke of the importance of making a commitment to community and family in daily life. "If you have a good community behind you and a good family supporting you, then, when the buck stops with you, there is the strength of that community and that family to draw upon."[16] She invited them as they go into their various careers, to join with her in rebuilding an environment through family and community, where children can grow into strong and constructive human beings.

> Somehow or other, we have got to be able to pursue the careers we have chosen . . . and make a commitment to the community—all the while remembering that the *family has got to come first.* Somehow or other, we have got to reorder our lives so that we can put family first every step of the way.[17]

Janet Reno's vision of building a better America through family and community has been an inspiration for many young people. The summer that Naseem Dhanani, a Cornell University senior, served as an intern in state attorney Reno's Dade County office, her law career plans had been focused on private practice, not government work. "But after I saw what kind of a woman Ms. Reno was, and how she was contributing to the community, I really learned a sense of giving something back to the community. . . . She's become a role model for me, and a lot of other women, too."[18]

With her unshakable belief that to build a better America we must start with children and family, Reno has sometimes been accused of being more a social worker than a prosecutor. But the true focus of her life remains in providing justice for all.

In the attorney general's conference room, on display near the American flag is the official flag of the attorney general. Its background is blue, with a white star near each corner. In the middle is the central design of the Department of Justice seal. This design bears the Latin motto: *Qui Pro Domina Justitia Sequitur* (Who prosecuted in behalf of our Lady Justice).[19] This motto appears to symbolize Attorney General Janet Reno.

Recently she was asked, "What gives you particular satisfaction or joy in your work as Attorney General?"

"To be able to serve the American people, in trying to make sure there is justice for all the people of this country," she replied.[20]

And all across America, people believe Attorney General Janet Reno is doing exactly that.

A Message From Janet Reno To America's Young People

✔ 1. Believe in yourself and the fact that you can do almost anything you want to do, if it is the right thing to do and you work hard at doing it.

✔ 2. Do and say what you believe to be right—not what you think people want to hear you say.

✔ 3. Study hard and prepare yourself by learning to read quickly and thoroughly; learn to write clearly and persuasively, and to understand computers and arithmetic. You will need a solid foundation on which to build.

✔ 4. Always remember that your family (and in the future your own children) is your most precious possession, and always remember to care for those you love.

✔ 5. Work hard but take time to enjoy the world and its people.

Chronology

1938—Janet Reno born on July 21, in Miami, Florida.
1944—Attends Dade County Public Schools in Miami.
-1956
1956—Wins Florida State High School Extemporaneous Speaking Contest; graduates, as valedictorian, from Coral Gables Senior High School.
1960—Graduates from Cornell University, with A.B. in chemistry.
1963—Graduates from Harvard Law School with LL.B.
1963—Works as associate in firm of Brigham and
-1967 Brigham in Miami.
1967—Henry Reno, her father, dies; becomes partner in Lewis and Reno in Miami.
1971—Becomes Staff Director for Judiciary Committee, Florida House of Representatives.
1972—Volunteers as Director of YWCA of Greater
-1974 Miami.
1973—Works as administrative assistant to state
-1976 attorney of Dade County, Florida.
1973—Volunteers as Director of Children & Family
-1975 Service Agency and Children's Psychiatric Center.
1976—Partner in Steel, Hector, and Davis in Miami.
-1978
1978—Serves as state attorney of Dade County.
-1993

1981—Presented Herbert Harley Award by the American Judicature Society.
1984—Becomes guardian of Daphne and Daniel Webb; elected president of Florida Prosecuting Attorney's Association.
1988—Inducted into Hall of Fame, Coral Gables Senior High School.
1992—Jane Wood Reno, her mother, dies.
1993—Appointed United States Attorney General, by President Bill Clinton; receives the Margaret Brent Women Lawyers of Achievement Award, from the American Bar Association's Commission on Women in the Profession; awarded Honorary Doctor of Laws degree from Barry University, Miami, Florida.
1994—Awarded Honorary Doctor of Humane Letters degree from University of Miami, in Miami, Florida.

Chapter Notes

Chapter 1

1. Holly Idelson, "Clinton's New Choice Is Reno: Search Din Dies Down," *Congressional Quarterly*, February 13, 1993, p. 321.

2. Holly Idelson, "Reno's Confirmation Was Easy: The Hard Work Lies Ahead," *Congressional Quarterly*, March 13, 1993, p. 601.

3. Ibid.

4. Martin Dyckman, "Janet Reno: 'Strong Enough To Take On the World'," *St. Petersburg Times*, March 14, 1993, p. 1D.

5. "Oath," *The World Book Encyclopedia*, Vol. 12 (Chicago: Field Enterprises Educational Corp., 1959), p. 5827.

6. "Reno Confirmed Unanimously By Senate As Attorney General," *Pensacola News Journal*, March 12, 1993, p. 2A.

Chapter 2

1. Jill Maunder, "They Call the State Attorney Miss," *Floridian*, January 14, 1979, p. 7.

2. "Everglades," *World Book Encyclopedia*, Vol. 5 (Chicago: Field Enterprises Educational Corp., 1959), p. 2420.

3. "Chickees Rise on Everglades Isle," *National Geographic*, Vol. 110, December 1956, p. 827.

4. Andy Taylor, "Calamity Jane," *Tropic*, March 11, 1979, pp. 40–46.

5. Laura Blumenfeld, "Janet Reno: Tower of Justice," *Cosmopolitan*, July 1993, p. 188.

6. Elaine Shannon, "The Unshakable Janet Reno," *Vogue*, August 1993, p. 262.

7. Nancy Gibbs, "Truth, Justice and the Reno Way," *Time*, July 12, 1993, p. 26.
8. Telephone interview with Maggy Hurchalla, May 5, 1994.
9. Gibbs, p. 23.
10. Interview by letter with Janet Reno, December 10, 1993.
11. Maggy Hurchalla interview.
12. Gibbs, p. 23.

Chapter 3

1. Interview by letter with Janet Reno, December 10, 1993.
2. Laura Blumenfeld, "Janet Reno: Tower of Justice," *Cosmopolitan*, July 1993, p. 188.
3. Robert Hardin, "Reno: Year One," *Tropic*, March 11, 1979, p. 15.
4. Ibid.
5. Lisa Bennett, "Clinton Taps Arts College Alumna To Serve As U.S. Attorney General," *Cornell '93*, Winter 1993, p. 10.
6. Hardin, p. 15.
7. Ibid.
8. Barbara Gordon, "Let's Not Mix Things Up," *Parade*, May 2, 1993, p. 5.
9. Ibid.
10. *Harvard Law School Admissions Booklet* (1993), p. 10.
11. Ibid.
12. Ibid.
13. Hardin, pp. 11–12.
14. *Harvard Law School Admissions Booklet*, p. 1.
15. Hardin, p. 11.

16. Gordon, p. 5.

17. Nancy Waring, "Janet Reno '63, Attorney General," *Harvard Law Bulletin*, June 1993, p. 13.

Chapter 4

1. Elaine Shannon, "The Unshakable Janet Reno," *Vogue*, August 1993, p. 262.

2. Martin Dyckman, "Janet Reno: 'Strong Enough To Take On the World'," *St. Petersburg Times*, March 13, 1993, p. 8D.

3. "Reno, Janet," *Current Biography Yearbook* (New York: H.W. Wilson Co., 1993), p. 486.

4. Dyckman, p. 9D.

5. Shannon, p. 262.

6. Laura Blumenfeld, "Janet Reno: Tower of Justice," *Cosmopolitan*, July 1993, p. 189.

7. Dyckman, p. 8D.

8. Janet Reno, "Performance Not Promises," Campaign Brochure, 1978, p. 2.

9. Ibid.

10. Ibid., p. 1.

Chapter 5

1. "Reno, Janet," *Current Biography Yearbook* (New York: H.W. Wilson Co., 1993), p. 487.

2. Ibid.

3. Laura Blumenfeld, "Janet Reno: Tower of Justice," *Cosmopolitan*, July 1993, p. 189.

4. Elaine Shannon, "The Unshakable Janet Reno," *Vogue*, August 1993, p. 262.

5. Andy Taylor, "Calamity Jane," *Tropic*, March 11, 1979, p. 48.

6. Blumenfeld, p. 188.

7. "Janet Reno's Solution To Crime: Take Care of the Toddlers," *The Pantagraph*, September 16, 1993, p. C-1.

8. "Hall of Fame Induction," *Highlights*, Coral Gables Senior High School, February 11, 1988, p. 1.

9. Margaria Fichtner, "Florida Loses A Pioneer," *Miami Herald*, December 22, 1992, p. 77.

Chapter 6

1. Elaine Shannon, "The Unshakable Janet Reno," *Vogue*, August 1993, p. 261.

2. Ibid.

3. Videotape of Attorney General Nomination, Purdue University Public Affairs Video Archives, February 11, 1993.

4. Ibid.

5. Ibid.

6. Laura Blumenfeld, "Janet Reno: Tower of Justice," *Cosmopolitan*, July 1993, p. 189.

7. Jill Mauder, "Janet Reno: She's Not a Typical State Attorney," *Floridian*, January 14, 1979, p. 7.

8. Videotape, February 11, 1993.

9. "Supreme Court Confirmation Process," *Chicago Tribune*, July 21, 1993, p. 8.

10. "Senate Judiciary Committee Hearing: Janet Reno, Attorney General Nominee," Library of Congress Transcript ID: 930645, March 9, 1993.

11. Ibid.

12. Ibid.

13. Ibid.

14. Martin Dyckman, "Janet Reno: Strong Enough To Take on the World," *St. Petersburg Times*, March 14, 1993, p. 1D.

15. "Remarks by President Bill Clinton at Swearing-In Ceremony for Janet Reno as Attorney General," Library of Congress transcript ID: 931020, March 12, 1993.

16. Ibid.

Chapter 7

1. "Legal Activities," United States Department of Justice Publication, 1992–1993, p. 21.

2. Ibid., p. 80.

3. Elaine Shannon, "The Unshakable Janet Reno," *Vogue*, August 1993, p. 313.

4. Ibid.

5. Richard Lacayo, "In the Grip of a Psychopath," *Time*, May 3, 1993, p. 34.

6. Ginny Carroll, et al., "Children of the Cult," *Newsweek*, May 17, 1993, pp. 48–50.

7. Nancy Gibbs, "Fire Storm in Waco," *Time*, May 3, 1993, p. 36.

8. Ibid., pp. 36–37.

9. Ibid., p. 30.

10. "Reno, Janet," *Current Biography Yearbook* (New York: H.W. Wilson Co., 1993), p. 489.

11. Shannon, p. 261.

12. Janet Reno interview with Larry King, CNN, aired April 19, 1993. Transcript Number 807.

13. Stanley W. Cloud, "Standing Tall," *Time*, May 10, 1993, p. 46.

14. Ibid., p. 47.

15. Michael Isikoff, "FBI Clashed Over Waco, Report Says," *The Washington Post*, October 9, 1993, p. A1.

16. Nicholas M. Horrock, "U.S. Vows to Redouble Fair-Lending Fight," *Chicago Tribune*, November 5, 1993, Sec. 3, p. 1.

17. Lynne Marek, "Reno: Limit Immigration Flood Tide," *Chicago Tribune*, February 4, 1994, p. 8.

18. "Reno Confirmed Unanimously by Senate as Attorney General," *Pensacola News Journal,* March 12, 1993.

19. Lynne Marek, "Schroeder Praises 103rd Congress," *Chicago Tribune*, December 26, 1993, Sec. 6, p. 1.

20. Mark Willen, "Clinton Picks Freeh for FBI," *Congressional Quarterly,* July 24, 1993, p. 1962.

21. Janet Reno introducing President Clinton at Swearing-In of FBI Director, C-SPAN, September 1, 1993.

Chapter 8

1. Don Colburn and Abigail Trafford, "Doctors Target Growing Epidemic of Violence," *The Washington Post,* October 12, 1993, p. 12.

2. Nancy Waring, "Janet Reno '63, Attorney General," *Harvard Law Bulletin,* June 1993, p. 13.

3. Janet Reno interview with Ted Koppel, "Gun Violence Against Kids," ABC News *Nightline,* aired June 7, 1993.

4. "Highlights of Bill," *The Washington Post,* November 25, 1993, p. A24.

5. "United States Constitution," *The World Book Encyclopedia,* Vol. 17, (Chicago: Field Enterprises Educational Corp., 1959), p. 8370.

6. Lawrence L. Knutson, "For Jim Brady, An Epic Battle Ends," *Commercial-News,* November 30, 1993, p. 8A.

7. TV News Column, *The Washington Post,* October 18, 1993, p. D26.

8. Ellen Edwards, "Reno: End TV Violence," *The Washington Post,* October 21, 1993, p. A1.

9. "Fox Leads TV Violence, Survey Says," *Chicago Tribune,* December 19, 1993.

10. Ibid.

11. "Reno Warns TV Industry to Curb Violence," *Congressional Quarterly,* October 23, 1993, p. 2885.

12. Janet Reno appearance at Senate Commerce Committee Hearing on TV Violence, *C-SPAN*, aired October 22, 1993.

13. Anna Quindlen, "Parents, Not TV, Must Be Responsible For Their Children," *Chicago Tribune*, October 29, 1993, Sec. 1. p. 11.

14. Nancy Gibbs, "Laying Down the Law," *Time*, August 23, 1993, p. 26.

15. Kevin Cullen, "Sportsmen Take Fire At Gun Ban Plans," *Commercial-News*, April 10, 1994, p. 8A.

16. Janet Reno interview on NBC's *Meet the Press*, aired January 23, 1994.

17. Richard Lacayo, "Wounding The Gun Lobby," *Time*, March 29, 1993, p. 30.

18. Gibbs, p. 23.

19. Andrew Gottesman, "Reno Says Social Problems Need Early Care," *Chicago Tribune*, July 19, 1994, Sec. 1, p. 3.

20. Elaine Shannon, "The Unshakable Janet Reno," *Vogue*, August 1993, p. 260.

Chapter 9

1. Nancy Gibbs, "Truth, Justice and the Reno Way," *Time*, July 12, 1993, p. 23.

2. Janet Reno interview with David Brinkley, ABC News, aired April 18, 1993. Transcript Number 599.

3. Nancy Waring, "Janet Reno '63, Attorney General," *Harvard Law Bulletin*, June 1993, p. 12.

4. Laura Blumenfeld, "Janet Reno: Tower of Justice," *Cosmopolitan*, July 1993, p. 187.

5. Ibid., p. 188.

6. Lisa Bennett, "Clinton Taps Arts College Alumna To Serve as U.S. Attorney General," *Cornell '93*, Winter 1993, p. 1.

7. Interview by letter with Janet Reno, December 10, 1993.

8. Janet Reno interview with Catherine Crier, ABC News, aired July 9, 1993. Transcript Number 1330.

9. Ibid.

10. Elaine Shannon, "The Unshakable Janet Reno," *Vogue*, August 1993, p. 260.

11. Ibid.

12. Nancy Gibbs, p. 22.

13. "Look Who Won Our Most Admired Women and Men Polls," *Good Housekeeping*, January 1994, p. 34.

14. Meg Laughlin, "Growing Up Reno," *Lears*, July 1993, p. 49.

15. "The Reluctant Star," *Newsweek*, May 17, 1993, p. 42.

16. Janet Reno, "Commencement Address At Barry University, Miami, Florida," May 10, 1993. Transcript, University Relations.

17. Ibid.

18. Bennett, p. 10.

19. *The World Book Encyclopedia*, Vol. 6, (Chicago: Field Enterprises Educational Corp., 1959), p. 2590d.

20. Interview by letter with Janet Reno, December 10, 1993.

Further Reading

Anderson, Paul. *Janet Reno: Doing the Right Thing.* New York: John Wiley & Sons, 1994.

Caplan, Lincoln. "Janet Reno's Choice." *The New York Times Magazine,* (May 15, 1994), 41ff.

Cloud, Stanley. "Standing Tall." *Time,* (May 10, 1993), 46.

Gibbs, Nancy. "Truth, Justice, and the Reno Way." *Time,* (July 12, 1993), 26.

Gordon, Barbara. "Let's Not Mix Things Up." *Parade Magazine,* (May 2, 1993), 5.

"The Reluctant Star." *Newsweek,* (May 17, 1993), 42.

"Reno, Janet." *Current Biography Yearbook.* New York: H.W. Wilson Co., 1993.

Index

A
abortion rights, 64, 85
Alcohol, Tobacco, and Firearms, Bureau of (ATF), 76
Americans with Disabilities Act, 82
Askew, Reubin, 41, 43
attorney general, 7, 73–74

B
Baird, Zoë, 60
Barry University, 111–112
Beavis and Butthead, 94
Biden, Joseph R., 67
Brady, James S., 92–93
Brady Law, 92–93
Brady, Sarah, 93
Branch Dividians, 76
Brigham and Brigham, 37
Brinkley, David, 102

C
Cisneros, Henry, 84
Clinton, Bill, 8, 9, 69, 77, 87, 96, 99
Clinton, Hillary Rodham, 60
Coral Gables High School, 20, 25, 57
Cornell University, 25–28, 31
crime, 8, 91–99
Crime Law, 99
Cuban exiles, 84–85

D
Dade County, Florida, 8, 45
D'Alemberte, Talbot "Sandy," 38
death penalty, 97
Department of Defense, 97
Dhanani, Naseem, 112
drug treatment, 51–52, 97

E
Everglades, 13–14

F
Fair Housing Act, 82
Federal Bureau of Investigation (FBI), 77, 78, 81–82, 87, 104, 105
Federal Communication Commission (FCC), 95–96
flag of the U.S. attorney general, 113
Florida Judiciary Committee, 38
Florida Senate Criminal Justice Committee, 41
Freedom of Access to Clinic Entrance Act, 85
Freeh, Louis J., 87, 89

G
Gelber, Seymour, 42
Germany, 20
Gernstein, Richard, 41, 43
Good Housekeeping, 111
Gore, Al, 64, 69
Graham, Robert "Bob," 69
Guinier, Lani, 110
gun control, 93, 97

H
Harvard Law School, 30–36, 102
House Judiciary Committee, 79
Hurchalla, Maggy, 18–20, 108

I
Immigration and Naturalization Services (INS), 82, 84–85

J
Justice Department, 7, 74, 79–81, 102, 104

K
Kennedy, Edward M., 85
Koresch, David, 76–78, 81

L
Larry King Live, 79
Lewis and Reno, 38
Lewis, Gerald, 38

M
Meet the Press, 97
"Message to America's Young People," 115
Miami Herald, 11, 13, 37, 67
Miami News, 11, 16
Miccosukee, 14–16

N
National Association for the Advancement of Colored People (NAACP), 53
National Parent-Teacher Association, 94
National Rifle Association, 93
Newsweek, 111
New York Newsday, 108
New York Times, The, 96, 111

O
Orr, John B., 41

P
police officers, 96, 99
Purdy, E. Wilson, 45

Q
Quindlen, Anna, 96

R
racial tension, 52–53
Rahman, Sheik Omar, 81–82
Reagan, Ronald, 93
Reno, Henry, 11–12, 29–30, 37–38
Reno, Janet,
attorney general confirmation, 69
attorney general nomination, 61
childhood, 11–23
college, 25–28
law school, 30–36
state attorney, 43–58, 59–60
Reno, Janet (niece), 9–10, 71
Reno, Jane Wood, 11–16, 26–27, 29, 31, 58, 107
Reno, Maggy, 12, 18–20, 108. *See also* Hurchalla, Maggy.
Reno, Mark, 12, 108
Reno, Robert, 12, 108
Rodham, Hugh, 59
Roe v. *Wade*, 64

S
Senate Commerce Committee, 94, 95
Senate Judiciary Committee, 60, 65, 67–69
Sessions, William, 77, 87
Smithsonian National Museum of Natural History, 107
Steel, Hector, and Davis, 42

T
television violence, 93–95

W
Waco, Texas, 76, 81
Webb, Daniel, 56, 108
Webb, Daphne, 56, 108
Webb, Frances, 56
White, Byron R., 10, 71
White House, 7, 8, 60, 78, 102
Women's Bar Association, 99
Wood, Daisy (aunt), 20
Wood, Daisy Sloan Hunter (grandmother), 19–20
Wood, George Washington, 30, 31
Wood, Kimba, 60
Wood, Winnie, 20
World Trade Center, 81